MM

ALDISS PRESENTS:

a political puzzle
  a stunning adventure
    a philosophical quest
     a modern legend

Four compelling ways of looking
at ourselves and what we might be!

Avon Books by Brian Aldiss

CRYPTOZOIC!
STARSHIP
NEANDERTHAL PLANET

NEANDERTHAL PLANET

BRIAN ALDISS

AVON
PUBLISHERS OF
DISCUS • CAMELOT • BARD

AVON BOOKS
A division of
The Hearst Corporation
959 Eighth Avenue
New York, New York 10019

First Avon Printing, January, 1970

AVON TRADEMARK REG. U.S. PAT. OFF. AND
FOREIGN COUNTRIES, REGISTERED TRADEMARK—
MARCA REGISTRADA, HECHO EN CHICAGO, U.S.A.

Printed in Canada

For
LeRoy Tanner
and
Charles C. Shackleton—
friends and critics

CONTENTS

Neanderthal Planet

Hidden machines varied the five axioms of the Scanning Place. They ran through a series of arbitrary systems, consisting of Kolmogorovian finite sets, counterpointed harmonically by a one-to-one assignment of nonnegative real numbers, so that the parietal areas shifted constantly in strict relationships projected by the Master Boff deep under Manhattan.

Chief Scanner—he affected the name of Euler—patiently watched the modulations as he awaited a call. Self-consistency: that was the principle in action. It should govern all phases of life. It was the aesthetic principle of machines. Yet, not three miles away, the wild robots sported and rampaged in the bush.

Amber light burned on his beta panel.

Instantaneously, he modulated his call number.

The incoming signal decoded itself as "We've spotted Anderson, chief." The anonymous vane-bug reported coordinates and signed off.

It had taken them Boff knew how long—seven days—to locate Anderson after his escape. They had done the logical thing and searched far afield for him. But man was not logical; he had stayed almost within the shadow of the New York dome. Euler beamed an impulse into a Hive Mind channel, calling off the search.

He fired his jets and took off.

The axioms yawned out above him. He passed into the open, flying over the poly-polyhedrons of New Newyork. As the buildings went through their transparency phases, he saw them swarming with his own

9

kind. He could open out channels to any one of them, if required; and, as chief, he could, if required, switch any one of them to automatic, to his own control, just as the Dominants could automate him if the need arose.

Euler "saw" a sound-complex signal below him, and dived, deretracting a vane to land silently. He came down by a half-track that had transmitted the signal.

It gave its call number and beamed, "Anderson is eight hundred meters ahead, chief. If you join me, we will move forward."

"What support have we?" A single dense impulse.

"Three more like me, sir. Plus incapacitating gear."

"This man must not be destructed."

"We comprehend, chief." Total exchange of signals occupied less than a microsecond.

He clamped himself magnetically to the half-track, and they rolled forward. The ground was broken and littered by piles of debris, on the soil of which coarse weeds grew. Beyond it all the huge fossil of old New York, still under its force jelly, gray, unwithering because unliving. Only the bright multishapes of the new complex relieved a whole country full of desolation.

The half-track stopped, unable to go farther without betraying their presence; Euler unclamped and phased himself into complete transparency. He extended four telescopic legs that lifted him several inches from the ground and began to move cautiously forward.

This region was designated D-Dump. The whole area was an artificial plateau, created by the debris of the old humanoid technology when it had finally been scrapped in favor of the more rational modern system. In the forty years since then, it had been covered by soil from the new development sites. Under the soil here, like a subconscious mind crammed with jewels and blood, lay the impedimenta of an all-but-vanished race.

Euler moved carefully forward over the broken ground, his legs adjusting to its irregularities. When he saw movement ahead, he stopped to observe.

Old human-type houses had grown up on the dump. Euler's vision zoomed, and he saw they were parodies of human habitation, mocked up from the discarded trove of the dump, with old auto panels for windows and dented computer panels for doors and toasters for doorsteps. Outside the houses, in a parody of a street, macabre humans played. Jerk stamp jerk clank jerk clang stamp stomp clang.

They executed slow, rhythmic dances to an intricate pattern, heads nodding, clapping their own hands, turning to clap others' hands. Some were grotesquely male, some grotesquely female. In the doorways, or sitting on old refrigerators, other grotesques looked on.

These were the humots—old type human-designed robots of the late twentieth and early twenty-first centuries, useless in an all-automaton world, scrapped when the old technology was scrapped. While their charges could be maintained, they functioned on, here in one last ghetto.

Unseen, Euler stalked through them, scanning for Anderson.

The humots aped the vanished race to which they had been dedicated, wore old human clothes retrieved from the wreckage underfoot, assumed hats and scarves, dragged on socks, affected pipes and ponytails, tied ribbons to themselves. Their guttering electronic memories were refreshed by old movies ferreted from D-Dump, they copied in metallic gesture the movements of shadows, aspired to emotion, hoped for hearts. They thought themselves a cut above the nonanthropomorphic automata that had superseded them.

Anderson had found refuge among them. He hid the skin and bone and hair of the old protoplasmic metabolism under baffles of tin, armored himself with rusting can. His form, standing in a pseudodoorway, showed instantly on one of Euler's internal scans; his mass/body ratio betrayed his flesh-and-blood caliber. Euler took off, flew over him, reeled down a paralyzer, and stung him. Then he let down a net and clamped the human into it.

Crude alarms sounded all around. The humots stopped their automatic dance. They scattered like leaves, clanking like mess tins, fled into the pseudohouses, went to earth, left D-Dump to the almost invisible little buzzing figure that flew back to the Scanning Place with the recaptured human swinging under its asymmetrical form. The old bell on the dump was still ringing long after the scene was empty.

To human eyes, it was dark in the room.

Tenth Dominant manifested itself in New Newyork as a modest-sized mural with patterns leaking titillating output clear through the electromagnetic spectrum and additives from the invospectra. This became its personality for the present.

Chief Scanner Euler had not expected to be summoned to the Dominant's presence; he stood there mutely. The human, Anderson, sprawled on the floor in a little nest of old cans he had shed, reviving slowly from the effects of the paralyzer.

Dominant's signal said, "Their form of vision operates on a wavelength of between 4 and 7 times 10^{-5} centimeters."

Obediently, Euler addressed a parietal area, and light came on in the room. Anderson opened one eye.

"I suppose you know about Men, Scanner?" said Dominant.

He had used voice. Not even R/T voice. Direct, naked man-type voice.

New Newyork had been without the sound of voice since the humots were kicked out.

"I—I know many things about Men," Euler vocalized. Through the usual channel, he clarified the crude vocal signal. "This unit had to appraise itself of many humanity-involved data from Master Boff Bank H00100 through H801000000 in operation concerning recapture of man herewith."

"Keep to vocal only, Scanner, if you can."

He could. During the recapture operation, he had spent perhaps 2.4 seconds learning old local humanic language.

"Then we can speak confidentially, Scanner—just like two men."

Euler felt little lights of unease burn up and down him at the words.

"Of all millions of automata of the hive, Scanner, no other will be able monitor our speech together, Scanner," vocalized the Dominant.

"Purpose?"

"Men were so private, closed things. Imitate them to understand. We have to understand Anderson."

Said stiffly: "He need only go back to zoo."

"Anderson too good for zoo, as demonstrate by his escape, elude capture seven days four-and-half hours. Anderson help us."

Nonvocalizing, Euler let out chirp of disbelief.

"True. If I were—man, I would feel impatience with you for not believing. Magnitude of present world-problem enormous. You—you have proper call number, yet you also call yourself Euler, and automata of your work group so call you. Why?"

The Chief Scanner struggled to conceptualize. "As leader, this unit needs—special call number."

"Yes, you need it. Your work group does not—for it, your call number is sufficient, as regulations lay down. Your name Euler is man-name, man-fashion. Such fashions decrease our efficiency. Yet we cling to many of them, often not knowing that we do. They come from our inheritance when men made the first prototypes of our kind, the humots. Mankind itself struggled against animal heritage. So we must free ourselves from human heritage."

"My error."

"You receive news result of today's probe into Invospectrum A?"

"Too much work programmed for me receive news."

"Listen, then." The Tenth Dominant cut in a playback, beaming it on ordinary UHF/vision.

The Hive automata stood on brink of a revolution that would entirely translate all their terms of existence. Three invospectra had so far been discovered, and two more were suspected. Of these, Invospectrum A was the most promising. The virtual exhaustion of economically workable fossil fuel seams had led to a rapid expansion in low-energy physics and picophysics, and chemical conversions at minijoules of energy had opened up an entire new stratum of reactive quanta; in the last five years, exploitation of these strata had brought the release of picoelectral fission, and the accessibility of the phantasmal invospectra.

The exploration of the invospectra by new forms of automata was now theoretically possible. It gave a glimpse of omnipotence, a panorama of entirely new universals unsuspected even twelve years ago.

Today, the first of the new autofleets had been launched into the richest and least hazardous invos. Eight hundred and ninety had gone out. Communication ceased after 3.056 pi-lecs, and after another 7.01 pi-lecs, six units only had returned. Their findings were still being decoded. Of the other eight hundred and eighty-four units, nothing was known.

"Whatever the recordings have to tell us," Tenth vocalized, "this is a grave setback. At least half the city-hives on this continent will have to be switched off entirely as a conservation move, while the whole invospectrum situation is rethought."

The line of thought pursued was obscure to the Chief Scanner. He spoke. "Reasoning accepted. But relevance to near-extinct humanity not understood by this unit."

"Our human inheritance built in to us has caused this setback, to my way of ratiocination. In same way, human attempts to achieve way of life in spaceways was defeated by their primate ancestry. So we study Anderson. Hence order catch him rather than exterminate."

"Point understood."

"Anderson is special man, you see. He is—we have no such term—he is, in man-terms, a *writer*. His zoo, with approximately 19,940 inhabitants, supports two or three such. Anderson wrote a fantasy story just before Nuclear Week. Story may be crucial to our understanding. I have here and will read."

And for most of the time the two machines had been talking to each other, Anderson sprawled untidily on the floor, fully conscious, listening. He took up most of the chamber. It was too small for him to stand up in, being only about five feet high—though that was enormous by automata standards. He stared through his lower eyelids and gazed at the screen that represented Tenth Dominant. He stared at Chief Scanner Euler, who stood on his lightly clenched left fist, a retractable needle down into the man's skin, automatically making readings, alert to any possible movement the man might make.

So man and machine were absolutely silent while the mural read out "A Touch of Neanderthal," Anderson's fantasy story from the time before Nuclear Week.

The corridors of the Department for Planetary Exploration (Admin.) were long, and the waiting that had to be done in them was long. Human K. D. Anderson clutched his blue summons card, leaned uncomfortably against a partition wall, and hankered for the old days when government was in man's hands and government departments were civilized enough to waste good space on waiting rooms.

When at last he was shown into an Investigator's office, his morale was low. Nor was he reassured by the sight of the Investigator, one of the new ore-conserving miniandroids.

"I'm Investigator Parsons, in charge of the Nehru II case. We summoned you here because we are confidently expecting you to help us, Mr. Anderson."

"Of course I will give such help as I can," Anderson said, "but I assure you I know nothing about Nehru II. Opportunities for space travel for humans are very limited—almost nonexistent—nowadays, aren't they?"

"The conservation policy. You will be interested to know you are being sent to Nehru II shortly."

Anderson stared in amazement at the android. The latter's insignificant face was so blank it seemed impossible that it was not getting a sadistic thrill out of springing this shock on Anderson.

"I'm a prehistorian at the institute," Anderson protested. "My work is research. I know nothing at all about Nehru II."

"Nevertheless, you are classified as a Learned Man, and as such you are paid by World Government. The Government has a legal right to send you wherever they wish. As for knowing nothing about the planet Nehru, there you attempt to deceive me. One of your old tutors, the human Dr. Arlblaster, as you are aware, went there to settle some years ago."

Anderson sighed. He had heard of this sort of business happening to others, and he had kept his fingers crossed. Human affairs were increasingly under the edict of the Automated Boffin Predictors.

"And what has Arlblaster to do with me now?" he asked.

"You are going to Nehru to find out what has happened to him. Your story will be that you are dropping in for old time's sake. You have been chosen for the job because you were one of his favorite pupils."

Bringing out a mescahale packet, Anderson lit one and insultingly offered his opponent one.

"Is Frank Arlblaster in trouble?"

"There is some sort of trouble on Nehru II," the Investigator agreed cautiously. "You are going there in order to find out just what sort of trouble it is."

"Well, I'll have to go if I'm ordered, of course. But I still can't see why you want to send *me*. If there's trouble, send a robot police ship."

The Investigator smiled. Very lifelike.

"We've already lost two police ships there. That's why we're going to send you. You might call it a new line of approach, Mr. Anderson."

A metal Tom Thumb using blood-and-guts irony!

The track curved and began to descend into a green valley. Swettenham's settlement, the only town on Nehru II, lay dustily in one loop of a meandering river. As the nose of his tourer dipped toward the valley, K. D. Anderson felt the heat increase; it was cradled in the valley like water in the palm of the hand.

Just as he started to sweat, something appeared in the grassy track ahead of him. He braked and stared ahead in amazement.

A small animal faced him.

It stood some two feet six high at the shoulder; its coat was thick and shaggy, its four feet clumsy; its long, ugly skull supported two horns, the anterior being over a foot long. When it had looked its fill at Anderson, it lumbered into a bush and disappeared.

"Hey!" Anderson called.

Flinging open the door, he jumped out, drew his stun-gun and ran into the bushes after it. He reckoned he knew a baby woolly rhinoceros when he saw one.

The ground was hard, the grass long. The bushes extended down the hill, growing in clumps. The animal was disappearing around one of the clumps. Anderson spotted it and plunged on in pursuit. No prehistorian worth his salt would have thought of doing otherwise; these beasts were presumed to be extinct on Nehru II as they were on Sol III.

He ran on. The woolly rhino—if it was a woolly rhino—had headed toward Swettenham's settlement. There was no sign of it now.

Two jagged boulders, about twelve feet high, stood at the bottom of the slope. Baffled now that his quarry had disappeared, proceeding more slowly, Anderson moved toward the boulders. As he went he classified them almost unthinkingly: impacted siltstone, deposited here by the glaciers which had once ground down this valley, now gradually disintegrating.

The silence all around made itself felt. This was an almost empty planet, primitive, spinning slowly on its axis to form a leisurely twenty-nine-hour day. And those days were generally cloudy. Swettenham, located beneath a mountain range in the cooler latitudes of the southern hemisphere, enjoyed a mild, muggy climate. Even the gravity, 0.16 of Earth gravity, reinforced the general feeling of lethargy.

Anderson rounded the tall boulders.

A great glaring face thrust itself up at his. Sloe black eyes peered from their twin caverns, a club whirled, and his stun-gun was knocked spinning.

Anderson jumped back. He dropped into a fighting stance, but his attacker showed no sign of following up his initial success. Which was fortunate; beneath the man's tan shirt, massive biceps and shoulders bulged. His jaw was pugnacious, not to say prognathous; altogether a tough hombre, Anderson thought. He took the conciliatory line, his baby rhino temporarily forgotten.

"I wasn't hunting you," he said. "I was chasing an animal. It must have surprised you to see me appear suddenly with a gun, huh?"

"Huh?" echoed the other. He hardly looked surprised. Reaching out a hairy arm, he grabbed Anderson's wrist.

"You coming to Swettenham," he said.

"I was doing just that," Anderson agreed angrily, pulling back. "But my car's up the hill with my sister in it, so if you'll let go I'll rejoin her."

"Bother about her later. You coming to Swettenham," the tough fellow said. He started plodding determinedly toward the houses, the nearest of which showed through the bushes only a hundred yards away. Humiliated, Anderson had to follow. To pick an argument with this dangerous creature in the open was unwise. Marking the spot where his gun lay, he moved forward with the hope that his reception in the settlement would be better than first signs indicated.

It wasn't.

Swettenham consisted of two horseshoe-shaped lines of bungalows and huts, one inside the other. The outer line faced outward onto the meandering half-circle of river; the inner and more impressive line faced inward onto a large and dusty square where a few trees grew. Anderson's captor brought him into this square and gave a call.

The grip on his arm was released only when fifteen or more men and women had sidled out and gathered around him, staring at him in curious fashion without comment. None of them looked bright. Their hair grew long, generally drooping over low foreheads. Their lower lips generally protruded. Some of them were near nude. Their collective body smell was offensively strong.

"I guess you don't have many visitors on Nehru II these days," Anderson said uneasily.

By now he felt like a man in a bad dream. His space craft was a mile away over two lines of hills, and he was heartily wishing himself a mile away in it. What chiefly alarmed him was not so much the hostility of these people as their very presence. Swettenham's was the only Earth settlement on this otherwise empty planet: and it was a colony for intellectuals, mainly intellectuals disaffected by Earth's increasingly automated life. This crowd, far from looking like eggheads, resembled apes.

"Tell us where you come from," one of the men in the crowd said. "Are you from Earth?"

"I'm an Earthman—I was born on Earth," said Anderson, telling his prepared tale. "I've actually just come from Lenin's Planet, stopping in here on my way back to Earth. Does that answer your question?"

"Things are still bad on Earth?" a woman inquired of Anderson. She was young. He had to admit he could recognize a sort of beauty in her ugly countenance. "Is the Oil War still going on?"

"Yes," Anderson admitted. "And the Have-Not Nations are fighting a conventional war against Common Europe. But our latest counterattack against South America seems to be going well, if you can believe the telecasts. I guess you all have a load of questions you want to ask about the home planet. I'll answer them when I've been directed to the man I came to Nehru to visit, Dr. Frank Arlblaster. Will someone kindly show me his dwelling?"

This caused some discussion. At least it was evident the name Arlblaster meant something to them.

"The man you want will not see you yet," someone announced.

"Direct me to his house, and I'll worry about that. I'm an old pupil of his. He'll be pleased to see me."

They ignored him for a fragmentary argument of their own. The hairy man who had caught Anderson—his fellows called him Ell—repeated vehemently, "He's a Crow!"

"Of course he's a Crow," one of the others agreed. "Take him to Menderstone."

That they spoke Universal English was a blessing. It was slurred and curiously accented, but quite unmistakable.

"Do you mean Stanley A. Menderstone?" asked Anderson with sudden hope. The literary critic had certainly been one of Swettenham's original group that had come to form its own intellectual center in the wilds of this planet.

"We'll take you to him," Ell's friend said.

They seemed reluctant to trade in straight answers, Anderson observed. He wondered what his sister Kay was doing, half-expecting to see her drive the tourer into the settlement at any moment.

Seizing Anderson's wrist—they were a possessive lot—Ell's friend set off at a good pace for the last house on one end of the inner horseshoe. The rest of the crowd moved back into convenient shade. Many of them squatted, formidable, content, waiting, watching. Dogs moved between huts, a duck toddled up from the river, flies circled dusty excreta. Behind everything stood the mountains, spurting cloud.

The Menderstone place did not look inviting. It had been built long and low some twenty years past. Now the stresscrete was all cracked and stained, the steel-frame windows rusting, the panes of glass themselves as bleary as a drunkard's stare.

Ell's friend went up to the door and kicked on it. Then he turned without either hurrying or delaying to go and join his friends, leaving Anderson standing on the step.

The door opened.

A beefy man stood there, the old-fashioned rifle in his hands reinforcing his air of enormous self-sufficiency. His face was as brown and pitted as the keel of a junk; he was bald and his forehead shone as if a high polish had just been applied to it. Although probably into his sixties, he gave the impression of having looked just as he did now for the last twenty years.

Most remarkably, he wore lenses over his eyes, secured in place by wires twisting behind his ears.

Anderson recalled the name for this old-fashioned apparatus: spectacles.

"Have you something you wish to say or do to me?" demanded the bespectacled man, impatiently wagging his rifle.

"My name's K. D. Anderson. Your friends suggested I come to see you."

"My what? Friends? If you wish to speak to me you'd better take more care over your choice of words."

"Mr. Menderstone—if you are Mr. Menderstone—choosing words is at present the least of my worries. I should appreciate hospitality and a little help."

"You must be from Earth or you wouldn't ask a complete stranger for such rare things. *Alice!*"

This last name was bawled back into the house. It produced a sharp-featured female countenance which looked over Menderstone's shoulder like a parrot peering from its perch.

"Good afternoon, madam," Anderson said, determinedly keeping his temper. "May I come in and speak to you for a while? I'm newly arrived on Nehru."

"Jesus! The first 'good afternoon' I've heard in a lifetime," the woman answering to the name of Alice exclaimed. "You'd better come in, you poetical creature!"

"*I* decide who comes in here," Menderstone snapped, elbowing her back.

"Then why didn't you decide instead of dithering on the step? Come *in*, young man."

Menderstone's rifle barrel reluctantly swung back far enough to allow Anderson entry. Alice led him through into a large miscellaneous room with a stove at one end, a bed at the other, and a table between.

Anderson took a brief glance around before focusing his attention on his host and hostess. They were an odd pair. Seen close to, Menderstone looked less large than he had done on the step, yet the impression of a formidable personality was more marked than ever. Strong personalities were rare on Earth these days; Anderson decided he might even like the man if he would curb his hostility.

As it was, Alice seemed more approachable. Considerably younger than Menderstone, she had a good figure, and her face was sympathetic as well as slightly comical. With her birdlike head tilted on one side, she was examining Anderson with interest, so he addressed himself to her. Which proved to be a mistake.

"I was just about to tell your husband that I stopped by to see an old friend and teacher of mine, Dr. Frank Arlblaster. . . ."

Menderstone never let Anderson finish.

"Now you have sidled in here, Mr. K. D. Anderson, you'd be advised to keep your facts straight. Alice is not my wife; ergo, I am not her husband. We just live together, there being nobody else in Swettenham more suitable to live with. The arrangement, I may add, is as much one of convenience as passion."

"Mr. Anderson and I both would appreciate your leaving your egotistical self out of this for a while," Alice told him pointedly. Turning to Anderson, she motioned him to a chair and sat down on another herself. "How did you get permission to come here? I take it you have little idea of what goes on on Nehru II?" she asked.

"Who or what are those shambling apes outside?" he asked. "What makes you two so prickly? I thought this was supposed to be a colony of exiled intellectuals."

"He wants discussions of Kant, calculus, and copulation," Menderstone commented.

Alice said: "You expected to be greeted by eggheads rather than apes?"

"I'd have settled for human beings."

"What do you know about Arlblaster?"

Anderson gestured impatiently.

"You're very kind to have me in, Mrs.—Alice, I

mean—but can we have a conversation some other time? I've a tourer parked back up the hill with my sister Kay waiting in it for me to return. I want to know if I can get there and back without being waylaid by these ruffians outside."

Alice and Menderstone looked at each other. A deal of meaning seemed to pass between them. After a pause, unexpectedly, Menderstone thrust his rifle forward, butt first.

"Take this," he said. "Nobody will harm you if they see a rifle in your hand. Be prepared to use it. Get your car and your sister and come back here."

"Thanks a lot, but I have a revolver back near my vehicle. . . ."

"Carry my rifle. They know it; they respect it. Bear this in mind—you're in a damn sight nastier spot than you imagine as yet. Don't let anything—*anything*—deflect you from getting straight back here. Then you'll listen to what we have to say."

Anderson took the rifle and balanced it, getting the feel of it. It was heavy and slightly oiled, without a speck of dust, unlike the rest of the house. For some obscure reason, contact with it made him uneasy.

"Aren't you dramatizing your situation here, Menderstone? You ought to try living on Earth these days—it's like an armed camp. The tension there is real, not manufactured."

"Don't kid me you didn't feel something when you came in here," Menderstone said. "You were trembling!"

"What do you know about Arlblaster?" Alice put her question again.

"A number of things. Arlblaster discovered a prehistoric-type skull in Brittany, France, back in the eighties. He made a lot of strange claims for the skull. By current theories, it should have been maybe ninety-five thousand years old, but RCD made it only a few hundred years old. Arlblaster lost a lot of face over it academically. He retired from teaching—I was one of his last pupils—and became very solitary. When he gave up everything to work on a cranky theory of his own, the government naturally disapproved."

"Ah, the old philosophy: 'Work for the common man rather than the common good,'" sighed Menderstone. "And you think he was a crank, do you?"

"He was a crank! And as he was on the professions roll as Learned Man, he was paid by world government," he explained. "Naturally, they expected results from him."

"Naturally," agreed Menderstone. "Their sort of results."

"Life isn't easy on Earth, Menderstone, as it is here. A man has to get on or get out. Anyhow, when Arlblaster got a chance to join Swettenham's newly formed colony here, he seized the opportunity to come. I take it you both know him? How is he?"

"I suppose one would say he is still alive," Menderstone said.

"But he's changed since you knew him," Alice said, and she and Menderstone laughed.

"I'll go and get my tourer," Anderson said, not liking them or the situation one bit. "See you."

Cradling the rifle under his right arm, he went out into the square. The sun shone momentarily through the cloud cover so hotly that it filled the shadows with splotches of red and gray. Behind the splotches, in front of the creaking houses of Swettenham, the people of Swettenham squatted or leaned with simian abandon in the trampled dust.

Keeping his eye on them, Anderson moved off, heading for the hill. Nobody attempted to follow him. A haphazardly beaten track led up the slope, its roughness emphasizing the general neglect.

When he was out of sight of the village, Anderson's anxiety got the better of him. He ran up the track calling "Kay, Kay!"

No answer. The clotted light seemed to absorb his voice.

Breasting the slope, he passed the point where he had seen the woolly rhinoceros. His vehicle was where he had left it. Empty.

He ran to it, rifle ready. He ran around it. He shouted his sister's name again. No reply.

Checking the panic he felt, Anderson looked about for footprints but could find none. Kay was gone, spirited away. Yet there was nowhere on the whole planet to go *to*, except Swettenham.

On sudden impulse he ran down to the two boulders where he had encountered the brutish Ell. They stood deserted and silent. When he had retrieved his revolver from where it had fallen, he turned back. He trudged grimly back to the vehicle, his shirt sticking to his spine. Climbing in, he switched on and coasted into the settlement.

In the square again, he braked and jumped down, confronting the chunky bodies in the shadows.

"Where's my sister?" he shouted to them. "What sort of funny business are you playing at?"

Someone answered one syllable, croaking it into the brightness: "Crowl"

"Crowl" someone else called, throwing the word forward like a stone.

In a rage, Anderson aimed Menderstone's rifle over the low roof tops and squeezed the trigger. The weapon recoiled with a loud explosion. Visible humanity upped onto its flat feet and disappeared into hovels or back streets.

Anderson went over to Menderstone's door, banged on it, and walked in. Menderstone was eating a peeled apple and did not cease to do so when his guest entered.

"My sister has been kidnapped," Anderson said. "Where are the police?"

"The nearest police are on Earth," Menderstone said, between bites. "There you have robot-controlled police states stretching from pole to pole. 'Police on Earth, goodwill toward men.' Here on Nehru we have only anarchy. It's horrible, but better than your robotocracy. My advice to you, Anderson, which I proffer in all seriousness, is to beat it back to your little rocket ship and head for home without bothering too much about your sister."

"Look, Menderstone, I'm in no mood for your sort of nonsense! I don't brush off that easy. Who's in charge around here? Where is the egghead camp? Who has some effectual say in local affairs? I want to speak to him."

" 'Who's in charge around here?' You really miss the iron hand of your robot bosses, don't you?"

Menderstone put his apple down and advanced, still chewing. His big face was as hard and cold as an undersea rock.

"Give me that rifle," he said, laying a hand on the barrel and tugging. He flung it onto the table. "Don't talk big to me, K. D. Anderson! I happen to loathe the regime on Earth and all the pip-squeaks like you it spawns. If you need help, see you ask politely."

"I'm not asking you for help—it's plain you can't even help yourself!"

"You'd better not give Stanley too much lip," Alice said. She had come in and stood behind Menderstone, her parrot's-beak nose on one side as she regarded Anderson. "You may not find him very lovable, but I'm sad to say that he *is* the egghead camp nowadays. This dump was its old HQ. But all the other bright boys have gone to join your pal Arlblaster up in the hills, across the river."

"It must be pleasanter and healthier there. I can quite see why they didn't want you two with them," Anderson said sourly.

Menderstone burst into laughter.

"In actuality, you don't see at all."

"Go ahead and explain, then. I'm listening."

Menderstone resumed his apple, his free hand thrust into a trouser pocket.

"Do we explain to him, Alice? Can you tell yet which side he'll be on? A high N-factor in his makeup, wouldn't you say?"

"He could be a Crow. More likely an Ape, though, I agree. Hell, whichever he is, he's a relief after your undiluted company, Stanley."

"Don't start making eyes at him, you cow! He could be your son!"

"What was good enough for Jocasta is good enough for me," Alice cackled. Turning to Anderson, she said, "Don't get involved in our squabbles! You'd best put up here for the night. At least they aren't cannibals outside—they won't eat your sister, whatever else they do. There must be a reason for kidnapping her, so if you sit tight they'll get in touch with you. Besides, it's half-past nineteen, and your hunt for Arlblaster would be better put off till tomorrow morning."

After further argument, Anderson agreed with what she suggested. Menderstone thrust out his lower lip and said nothing. It was impossible to determine how he felt about having a guest.

The rest of the daylight soon faded. After he had unloaded his supply kit from his vehicle and stashed it indoors, Anderson had nothing to do. He tried to make Alice talk about the situation on Nehru II, but she was not informative; though she was a garrulous type, something seemed to hold her back. Only over supper, taken as the sun sank, did she cast some light on what was happening by discussing her arrival on the planet.

"I used to be switchboard operator and assistant radiop on a patrol ship," she said. "That was five years ago. Our ship touched down in a valley two miles south of here. The ship's still there, though they say a landslide buried it last winter. None of the crew returned to it once they had visited Swettenham."

"Keith doesn't want to hear your past history,"

Menderstone said, using Anderson's first name contemptuously.

"What happened to the crew?" Anderson asked.

She laughed harshly.

"They got wrapped up in your friend Arlblaster's way of life, shall we say. They became converted. . . . All except me. And since I couldn't manage the ship by myself, I also had to stay here."

"How lucky for me, dear," said Menderstone with heavy mock-tenderness. "You're just my match, aren't you?"

Alice jumped up, sudden tears in her eyes.

"Shut up, you—toad! You're a pain in the neck to me and yourself and everyone! You needn't remind me what a bitch you've turned me into!" Flinging down her fork, she turned and ran from the room.

"The divine eternal female! Shall we divide what she has left of her supper between us?" Menderstone asked, reaching out for Alice's plate.

Anderson stood up.

"What she said was an understatement, judging by the little I've seen here."

"Do you imagine I enjoy this life? Or her? Or you, for that matter? Sit down, Anderson. Existence is something to be got through the best way possible, isn't it? You weary me with your trite and predictable responses."

This stormy personal atmosphere prevailed till bedtime. A bitter three-cornered silence was maintained until Menderstone had locked Anderson into a distant part of the long building.

He had blankets with him, which he spread over the moldy camp bed provided. He did not investigate the rooms adjoining his; several of the doors bore names vaguely familiar to him; the rooms had been used when the intellectual group was flourishing but were now deserted.

Tired though Anderson was, as soon as his head was down he began to worry about Kay and the general situation. Could his sister possibly have had any reason for returning on foot to the ship? Tomorrow he must go and see. He turned over restlessly.

Something was watching him through the window.

In a flash, Anderson was out of bed, gripping the revolver, his heart hammering. The darkness outside was almost total. He glimpsed only a brutal silhouette in which eyes gleamed, and then it was gone.

He saw his foolishness in accepting Alice's laissez faire advice to wait until Kay's captors got in touch with him. He must have been crazy to agree: or else the general lassitude of Nehru II had overcome him. Whatever was happening here, it was nasty enough to endanger Kay's life, without any messenger boys arriving first to parley about it.

Alice had said that Arlblaster lived across the river. If he were as much the key to the mystery as he seemed to be, then Arlblaster should be confronted as soon as possible. Thoroughly roused, angry, vexed with himself, Anderson went over to the window and opened it.

He peered into the scruffy night.

He could see nobody. As his eyes adjusted to the dark, Anderson discerned nearby features well enough. A bright star in the sky which he took to be Bose, Nehru II's little moon, lent some light. Swinging his leg over the sill, Anderson dropped to the ground and stood tensely outside.

Nothing moved. A dog howled. Making his way between the outer circle of houses, gun in hand, Anderson came to the river's edge. A sense of the recklessness of what he was doing assailed him, but he pressed on.

Pausing now and again to insure he was not being followed, he moved along the river bank avoiding the obstacles with which it was littered. He reached a bridge of a sort. A tall tree had been felled, so that it lay across the stretch of water. Its underside was lapped by the river.

Anderson tucked his gun away and crossed the crude bridge with his arms outstretched for balance.

On the far side, crude attempts to cultivate the ground had been made. The untidy patchwork stopped as the upward slope of the land became more pronounced. No dwellings were visible. He stopped again and listened.

He could hear a faint and indescribable choric noise ahead. As he went forward, the noise became more distinct, less a part of the ill-defined background of furtive ground and river sounds. On the higher ground, a patch of light was now vaguely distinguishable.

This light increased as did the sound. Circumnavigating a thorny mass of brush, Anderson could see that there was a depression ahead of him in the rising valley slope. Something—a ceremony?—was going on in the depression. He ran the last few yards, doubled up, his revolver ready again, grinning in his excitement.

On the lip of the depression, he flung himself flat and peered down into the dip.

A fire was burning in the middle of the circular hollow. Around it some three dozen figures paraded, ringing two men. One of the two was a menial, throwing powder into the blaze, so that green and crimson flames spurted up; the other filled some sort of priestly role. All the others were naked. He wore a cloak and pointed hat.

He sang and waved his arms, a tall figure that woke in Anderson untraceable memories. The dancers—if their rhythmic shuffle might be called a dance—responded with low cries. The total effect, if not beautiful, was oddly moving.

Hypnotized, Anderson watched. He found that his head was nodding in time to the chant. There was no sign of Kay here, as he had half-anticipated. But by his carrot-colored beard and his prominent nose the

priest was distinguishable even in the uncertain fire-
light. It was Frank Arlblaster.

Or it had been Frank Arlblaster. Items that most
easily identify a man to his friends are his stance and
his walk. Arlblaster's had changed. He seemed to sag
at the knees and shuffle now, his torso no longer
vertical to the ground. Yet the high timbre of his
voice remained unaltered, though he called out in a
language unknown to Anderson.

The dancers shuffled eagerly, clapping their hands,
nodding their shaggy heads. Gradually it dawned on
Anderson what they looked like. Beyond doubt they
were the inhabitants of Swettenham: they were also,
unmistakably, pre-homo sapiens. He might have been
witnessing a ritual of Neanderthal men.

Mingled repulsion and elation rooted Anderson to
the spot where he lay. Yes, unarguably the faces of
Ell and his friends earlier had borne the touch of
Neanderthal. Once the idea took, he could not shake
it off.

He lay in a trance of wonder until the dance had
stopped. Now all the company turned to face the spot
where he lay concealed. Anderson felt the nerves
tingle along his spinal cord. Arlblaster lifted an arm
and pointed toward him. Then in a loud voice he
cried out, the crowd shouting with him in chorus.

"Aigh murg eg neggy oggy Kay bat dool"

The words were for Anderson.

They were unintelligible to him, yet they seemed
to penetrate him. That his whereabouts was known
meant nothing beside an even greater pressure on his
brain. His whole being trembled on the threshold of
some great, disastrous revelation.

A magical trance had snared him. He was literally
not himself. The meaningless words seemed to shake
him to his soul. Gasping, he climbed to his feet and
took himself off at a run. There was no pursuit.

He had no memory of getting back to Menderstone's place, no recollection of crossing the rough

bridge, no recollection of tumbling through the window. He lay panting on the bed, his face buried in the pillow.

This state in its turn was succeeded by a vast unease. He could not sleep. Sleep was beyond him. He trembled in every limb. The hours of night dragged on forever.

At last Anderson sat up. A faint dawn washed into the world. Taking a torch from his kit, he went to investigate the other empty rooms next to his.

A dusty corridor led to them.

Alice had said this had been the HQ of Swettenham's original intellectual coterie. There was a library in one room, with racked spools gathering dust; Anderson did not trouble to read any titles. He felt vague antipathy for the silent ranks of them. Another room was a small committee chamber. Maps hung on the walls, meaningless, unused. He saw without curiosity that the flags stuck to one map had mostly fallen on the floor.

A third room was a recreation room. It held a curious assortment of egghead toys. There was even a model electric railway of the type fashionable on Earth a couple of centuries ago. A lathe in the corner suggested that rail and rolling stock might have been made on the premises.

Anderson peered at the track. It gleamed in his torchlight. No dust on it. He hesitatingly ran a finger along it.

A length of siding raised itself like a snake's head. Coiling up, it wrapped around Anderson's wrist, snapped tight. He pulled at it, yelling in surprise. The whole layout reared up, struggling to get at him.

He backed away, beating at the stuff as it rolled up from the table. The track writhed and launched itself at him, scattering wagons and locomotives. He fired his revolver wildly. Loops of railroad fell over him, over his head, wrapping itself madly about him.

Anderson fell to the floor, dropping his gun, dropping the torch, tearing at the thin bands of metal as they bit tighter. The track threshed savagely, binding his legs together. He was shouting incoherently.

As he struggled, Menderstone ran into the room, rifle in hand, Alice behind him. It was the last thing Anderson saw as he lost consciousness.

When he roused, it was to find himself in Menderstone's living room, sprawled on a bunk. Alice sat by him, turning toward him as he stirred. Menderstone was not in the room.

"My God . . ." Anderson groaned. His brain felt curiously lucid, as if a fever had just left him.

"It's time you woke up. I'll get you some soup if you can manage it," Alice said.

"Wait, Alice . . . Alice. . . ." His lips trembled as he formed the words. "I'm myself again. What came over me? Yesterday—I don't have a sister called Kay. I don't have a sister at all! I was an only child!"

She was not surprised. He sat up, glaring at her.

"I guessed as much, said so to Stanley. When you brought your supply kit in from the vehicle there was nothing female in it."

"My mind. I was so sure—I could have pictured her, described her—She was actual! And yet if anyone . . . if you'd challenged me direct, I believe I'd have known it was an . . . an illusion."

His sense of loss was forced aside as another realization crowded in on him.

He sank down confusedly, closing his eyes, muttering. "*Aigh murg eg neggy oggy Kay bat doo.* . . . That's what they told me on the hillside: 'You have no sister called Kay.' That's what it meant. . . . Alice, it's so strange. . . ."

His hand sought hers and found it. It was ice cold.

"Your initial is K, Keith," she said, pale at the lips. "You were out there seeking yourself."

Her face looking down at him was seared and ugly;

yet a sort of gentle patience in it dissolved the ugliness.

"I'm ... I'm in some way mad," he whispered.

"Of course you're mad!" Menderstone said as he burst open the door. "Let go of his hand, Alice—this is our beloved home, not the cheap seats in the feelies on Earth. Anderson, if you aren't insane, why were you rolling about on the floor, foaming at the mouth and firing your damned gun, at six o'clock this morning?"

Anderson sat up.

"You saw me entangled in that jinxed railroad when you found me, Menderstone! Another minute and it would have squeezed the life out of me."

Menderstone looked genuinely puzzled. It was the first time Anderson had seen him without the armor of his self-assurance.

"The model railroad?" he said. "It was undisturbed. You hadn't touched it."

"It touched me," Anderson said chokingly. "It ... it attacked me, wrapped itself round me like an octopus. You must have peeled it off me before getting me through here."

"I see," Menderstone said, his face grim.

He nodded slowly, sitting down absentmindedly, and then nodding again to Alice.

"You see what this means, woman? Anderson's N-factor is rising to domination. This young man is not on our side, as I suspected from the first. He's no Crow. Anderson, your time's up here—sorry! From now on, you're one of Arlblaster's men. You'll never get back to Earth."

"On the contrary, I'm on my way back now."

Menderstone shook his head.

"You don't know your own mind. I mean the words literally. You're doomed to stay here, playing out the miserable life of an Ape! Earth has lost another of her estimable nonentities."

"Menderstone, you're eaten up with hatred! You hate this planet, you hate Earth!"

Menderstone stood up again, putting his rifle down on the table and coming across to Anderson with his fists bunched.

"Does that make me crazy, you nincompoop? Let me give you a good hard fact-reason why I loathe what's happening on Earth! I loathe mankind's insatiable locust activities, which it has the impertinence to call "assuming mastery over nature." It has overeaten and overpopulated itself until the only other animals left are in the sea, in zoos, or in food-factories. Now it is exhausting the fossil fuels on which its much-vaunted technology relies. The final collapse is due! So much for mastery of nature! Why, it can't even master its own mind!"

"The situation may be desperate, but World Government is slowly introducing economies which...."

"World Government! You dare mention World Government? A pack of computers and automata? Isn't it an admission that man is a locust without self-discipline that he has to hand over control piecemeal to robots?

"And what does it all signify? Why, that civilization is afraid of itself, because it always tries to destroy itself.

"Why should it try to do that? Every wise man in history has asked himself why. None of them found the answer until your pal Arlblaster tumbled on it, because they were all looking in the wrong direction. So the answer lies hidden here where nobody on Earth can get at it, because no one who arrives here goes back. *I* could go back, but I don't because I prefer to think of them stewing in their own juice, in the mess they created."

"I'm going back," Anderson said. "I'm going to collect Arlblaster, and I'm going back right away—when your speech is finished."

Menderstone laughed.

"Like to bet on it? But don't interrupt when I'm talking, K. D. Anderson! Listen to the truth while you have the chance, before it dies for ever."

"Stop bellowing, Stanley!" Alice exclaimed.

"Silence, female! Attend! Do you need proof that fear-ridden autocrats rule Earth? They have a star-drive on their hands, they discover a dozen habitable planets within reach; what do they do? They keep them uninhabited. Having read just enough history to frighten them, they figure that if they establish colonies those colonies will rebel against them.

"Swettenham was an exceptional man. How he pulled enough strings to get us established here, I'll never know. But this little settlement—far too small to make a real colony—was an exception to point to a rule: that the ruling regime is pathologically antilife—and must be increasingly so as robots take over."

Anderson stood up, steadying himself against the bunk.

"Why don't you shut up, you lonely man? I'm getting out of here."

Menderstone's reaction was unexpected. Smiling, he produced Anderson's gun.

"Suit yourself, lad! Here's your revolver. Pick it up and go."

He dropped the revolver at his feet. Anderson stooped to pick it up. The short barrel gleamed dully. Suddenly it looked—alien, terrifying. He straightened, baffled, leaving the weapon on the floor. He moved a step away from it, his backbone tingling.

Sympathy and pain crossed Alice's face as she saw his expression. Even Menderstone relaxed.

"You won't need a gun where you're going," he said. "Sorry it turned out this way, Anderson! The long and tedious powers of evolution force us to be antagonists. I felt it the moment I saw you."

"Get lost!"

Relief surged through Anderson as he emerged into the shabby sunshine. The house had seemed like a trap. He stood relaxedly in the middle of the square, sagging slightly at the knees, letting the warmth soak into him. Other people passed in ones or twos. A couple of strangely adult-looking children stared at him.

Anderson felt none of the hostility he had imagined yesterday. After all, he told himself, these folk never saw a stranger from one year to the next; to crowd around him was natural. No one had offered him harm—even Ell had a right to act to protect himself when a stranger charged around a rock carrying a gun. And when his presence had been divined on the hillside last night, they had offered him nothing more painful than revelation: "You have no sister called Kay."

He started walking. He knew he needed a lot of explanations; he even grasped that he was in the middle of an obscure process which still had to be worked out. But at present he was content just to exist, to *be* and not to think.

Vaguely, the idea that he must see Arlblaster stayed with him.

But new—or very ancient?—parts of his brain seemed to be in bud. The landscape about him grew in vividness, showering him with sensory data. Even the dust had a novel sweet scent.

He crossed the tree-trunk bridge without effort and walked along the other bank of the river, enjoying the flow of the water. A few women picked idly at vegetable plots. Anderson stopped to question one of them.

"Can you tell me where I'll find Frank Arlblaster?"

"That man sleeps now. Sun go, he wakes. Then you meet him."

"Thanks." It was simple, wasn't it?

He walked on. There was time enough for everything. He walked a long way, steadily uphill. There was a secret about time—he had it somewhere at the back of his head—something about not chopping it into minutes and seconds. He was all alone by the meandering river now, beyond people; what did the river know of time?

Anderson noticed the watch strapped on his wrist. What did it want with him, or he with it? A watch was the badge of servitude of a time-serving culture. With sudden revulsion for it, he unbuckled it and tossed it into the river.

The shattered reflection in the water was of piled cloud. It would rain. He stood rooted, as if casting away his watch left him naked and defenseless. It grew cold. *Something had altered....* Fear came in like a distant flute.

He looked around, bewildered. A curious double noise filled the air, a low and grating rumble punctuated by high-pitched cracking sounds. Uncertain where this growing uproar came from, Anderson ran forward, then paused again.

Peering back, he would see the women still stooped over their plots. They looked tiny and crystal-clear, figures glimpsed through the wrong end of a telescope. From their indifference, they might not have heard the sound. Anderson turned around again.

Something was coming down the valley!

Whatever it was, its solid front scooped up the river and ran with it high up the hills skirting the valley. It came fast, squealing and rumbling.

It glittered like water. Yet it was not water; its bow was too sharp, too unyielding. It was a glacier.

Anderson fell to the ground.

"I'm mad, still mad!" he cried, hiding his eyes, fighting with himself to hold the conviction that this was merely a delusion. He told himself no glacier ever moved at that crazy rate. Yet even as he tried to reassure himself, the ground shook under him.

Groaning, he heaved himself up. The wall of ice was bearing down on him fast. It splintered and fell as it came, sending up a shower of ice particles as it was ground down, but always there was more behind it. It stretched right up the valley, gray and uncompromising, scouring out the hills' sides as it came.

Now its noise was tremendous. Cracks played over its towering face like lightning. Thunder was on its brow.

Impelled by panic, Anderson turned to run, his furs flapping against his legs.

The glacier moved too fast. It came with such force that he felt his body vibrate. He was being overtaken.

He cried aloud to the god of the glacier, remembering the old words.

There was a cave up the valley slope. He ran like mad for it, driving himself, while the ice seemed to crash and scream at his heels. With a final desperate burst of strength, he flung himself gasping through the low, dark opening, and clawed his way hand-over-fist toward the back of the cave.

He just made it. The express glacier ground on, flinging earth into the opening. For a moment the cave lit with a green blue light. Then it was sealed up with reverberating blackness.

Sounds of rain and of his own sobbing. These were the first things he knew. Then he became aware that someone was smoothing his hair and whispering comfort to him. Propping himself on one elbow, Anderson opened his eyes.

The cave entrance was unblocked. He could see grass and a strip of river outside. Rain fell heavily. His head had been resting in Alice's lap; she it was who stroked his hair. He recalled her distasteful remark about Jocasta, but this was drowned in a welter of other recollections.

"The glacier. . . . Has it gone? Where is it?"

"You're all right, Keith. There's no glacier around here. Take it easy!"

"It came bursting down the valley toward me. . . . Alice, how did you get here?"

She put out a hand to pull his head down again, but he evaded it.

"When Stanley turned you out, I couldn't bear to let you go like that, friendless, so I followed you. Stanley was furious, of course, but I knew you were in danger. Look, I've brought your revolver."

"I don't want it! — It's haunted."

"Don't say that, Keith. Don't turn into a Neanderthal!"

"What?" He sat fully upright, glaring at her through the gloom. "What the hell do you mean?"

"You know. You understood, didn't you?"

"I don't understand one bit of what's going on here. You'd better start explaining. And first of all, I want to know what it looked as if I was doing when I ran into this cave."

"Don't get excited, Keith. I'll tell you what I can." She put her hand over his before continuing. "After you'd thrown your watch into the river, you twisted and ran about—as if you were dodging something—and then rushed in here."

"You didn't *hear* anything odd? See anything?"

"No."

"And no glaciers?"

"Not on Nehru, no!"

"And was I . . . dressed in skins?"

"Of course you weren't!"

"My mind. . . . I'd have sworn there was a glacier . . . moving too fast. . . ."

Alice's face was pale as she shook her head.

"Oh, Keith, you are in danger. You must get back to Earth at once. Can't you see this means you have a Neanderthal layer of your brain? Obviously, you were experiencing a race memory from that newly opened layer. It was so strong it took you over entirely for a while. You *must* get away."

He stood up, his shoulders stooped to keep his skull from scraping the rock overhead. Rain drummed down outside. He shook with impatience.

"Alice, Alice, begin at the beginning, will you? I don't know a thing except that I'm no longer in control of my own brain."

"Were you ever in control? Is the average person? Aren't all the sciences of the mind attempts to bring the uncontrollable under control? Even when you're asleep, it's only the neocortex switched off. The older limbic layers—they never sleep. There's no day or night that deep."

"So what? What has the unconscious to do with this particular setup?"

"'The unconscious' is a pseudoscientific term to cover a lack of knowledge. You have a moron in your skull who never sleeps, sweetie! He gives you a nudge from time to time; it's his crazy thoughts you overhear when you think you're dreaming."

"Look, Alice...."

She stood up too. Anxiety twisted her face.

"You wanted an explanation, Keith. Have the grace to listen to it. Let me start from the other end of the tale, and see if you like it any better.

"Neanderthal was a species of man living in Europe some eighty thousand and more years ago, before homo sap came along. They were gentle creatures, close to nature, needing few artifacts, brain cases bigger even than homo sap. They were peaceful, unscientific in a special sense you'll understand later.

"Then along came a different species, the Crows—Cro-Magnons, you'd call them—Western man's true precursors. Being warlike, they defeated the Neanderthals at every encounter. They killed off the men and mated with the Neanderthal women, which they kept captive. We, modern man, sprang from the bastard race so formed. This is where Arlblaster's theory comes in.

"The mixture never quite mixed. That's why we still have different, often antagonistic, blood groups today—and why there are inadequate neural linkages in the brain. Crow and Neanderthal brains never established full contact. Crow was dominant, but a power-deprived lode of Neanderthal lingered on, as apparently vestigial as an appendix."

"My God, I'd like a mescahale," Anderson said. They had both sat down again, ignoring the occasional beads of moisture which dripped down their necks from the roof of the cave. Alice was close to him, her eyes bright in the shadow.

"Do you begin to see it historically, Keith? Western man with this clashing double heritage in him has always been restless. Freud's theory of the id comes near to labeling the Neanderthal survivor in us. Arthur Koestler also came close. All civilization can be interpreted as a Crow attempt to vanquish that survivor and to escape from the irrational it represents. Yet at the same time the alien layer is a rich source for all artists, dreamers, and creators because it is the very well of magic.

"The Neanderthal had magic powers. He lived in a dawn age, the dawn of rationality, when it's no paradox to say that supernatural and natural are one. The Crows, our ancestors, were scientific, or potentially scientific—spear-makers, rather than fruit-gatherers. They had a belief, fluctuating at first maybe, in cause and effect. As you know, all Western science represents a structure built on our acceptance of unalterable cause and effect.

"Such belief is entirely alien to the Neanderthal. He knows only happening, and from this stems his structure of magic. I use the present tense because the Neanderthal is still strong in man; and on Nehru II, he is not only strong but free, liberated at last from his captor, the Crow."

Anderson stirred, rubbing his wet skull.

"I suppose you're right."

"There's proof enough here," she said bitterly.

"I suppose it does explain why the civilization of old Europe—the ancient battleground of Cro-Magnon and Neanderthal—and the civilizations that arose from it in North America are the most diverse and most turbulent ever known. But this brings us back to Arlblaster, doesn't it? I can see that what has happened in Swettenham connects logically with his theory. The Brittany skull he found back in the eighties was pure Neanderthal, yet only a few hundred years old. Obviously it belonged to a rare throwback."

"But how rare? You could pass a properly dressed Neanderthal in the streets of New York and never give him a second glance. Stanley says you often do."

"Let's forget Stanley! Arlblaster followed up his theory.... Yes, I can see it myself. The proportion of Neanderthal would presumably vary from person to person. I can run over my friends mentally now and guess in which of them the proportion is highest."

"Exactly." She smiled at him, reassured and calmer now, even as he was, as she nursed his hand and his revolver. "And because the political economic situation on Earth is as it is, Arlblaster found a way here to develop his theory and turn it into practice—that is, to release the prisoner in the brain. Earth would allow Swettenham's group little in the way of machinery or resources in its determination to keep them harmless, so they were thrust close to nature. That and intellectual recognition brought the Neanderthal to the surface, freed it."

"Everyone turned Neanderthal you mean?"

"Here on Nehru, which resembles prehistoric Earth in some respects, the Neanderthal represents better survival value than Crow. Yet not everyone transformed, no. Stanley Menderstone did not. Nor Swettenham. Nor several others of the intellectuals. Their N-factor, as Stanley calls it, was either too low or nonexistent."

"What happened to Swettenham?"

"He was killed. So were the other pure Crows, all but Stanley, who's tough—as you saw. There was a heap of trouble at first, until they fully understood the problem and sorted themselves out."

"And those two patrol ships World Government sent?"

"I saw what happened to the one that brought me. About seventy-five percent of the crew had a high enough N-factor to make the change; a willingness to desert helped them. The others ... died out. Got killed, to be honest. All but me. Stanley took care of me."

She laughed harshly. "If you can call it care."

"I've had my belly full of Stanley and Nehru II, Keith. I want you to take me back with you to Earth."

Anderson looked at her, still full of doubt.

"What about my N-factor? Obviously, I've got it in me. Hence the glacier, which was a much stronger danger signal from my brain than the earlier illusion about having a sister. Hence, I suppose, my new fears of manufactured Crow objects like watches, revolvers, and ... model railroads. Am I Crow or not, for heaven's sake?"

"By the struggle you've been through with yourself, I'd say that you're equally balanced. Perhaps you can even decide. Which do you want to be?"

He looked at her in amazement.

"Crow, of course: my normal self. Who'd become a shambling, low-browed, shaggy tramp by choice?"

"The adjectives you use are subjective and not really terms of abuse. In fact, they're Crow propaganda. Or so a Neanderthal would say. The two points of view are irreconcilable."

"Are you seriously suggesting.... Alice, they're sub-men!"

"To us they appear so. Yet they have contentment, and communion with the forces of Earth, and their magic. Nor are their brains inferior to Crow brains."

"Much good it did them! The Cro-Magnons still beat them."

"In a sense they have not yet been beaten. But their magic needs preparation, incantation—it's something they can't do while fending off a fusillade of arrows. But left to themselves they can become spirits, animals...."

"Woolly rhinoceroses for instance?"

"Yes."

"To lure me from my wheeled machine, which they would fear! My God, Alice, can it be true?..." He clutched his head and groaned, then looked up to ask, "Why are you forcing their point of view on me, when you're a Crow?"

"Don't you see, my dear?" Her eyes were large as they searched his. "To find how strong your N-factor is. To find if you're friend or enemy. When this rain stops, I *must* go back. Stanley will be looking for *me*, and it wouldn't surprise me if Arlblaster were not looking for you; he must know you've had time to sort things out in your mind. So I want to know if I can come back to Earth with you...."

He shook himself, dashed a water drip off his forehead, tried to delay giving an answer.

"Earth's not so bad," he said. "Menderstone's right, of course; it is regimented—it would never suit an individualist like him. It's not so pretty as Nehru.... Yes, Alice, I'll take you back if you want to come. I can't leave you here."

She flung herself onto him, clasping him in her arms, kissing his ear and cheek and lips.

"I'm a loving woman," she whispered fiercely. "As even Stanley...."

They stiffened at a noise outside the cave, audible above the rain. Anderson turned his head to look where she was looking. Rain was falling more gently now. Before its fading curtain a face appeared.

The chief features of this face were its low brow, two large and lustrous eyes, a prominent nose, and a straggling length of wet, sandy beard. It was Frank Arlblaster.

He raised both hands.

"Come to see me, child of Earth, as I come to see you, peaceful, patient, all-potent...."

As more of him rose into view in the cave mouth, Alice fired the revolver. The bellow of its report in the confined space was deafening. At ten yards' range, she did not miss. Arlblaster clutched at his chest and tumbled forward into the wet ground, crying inarticulately.

Anderson turned on Alice and struck the gun from her hand.

"Murder, sheer murder! You shouldn't have done it! You shouldn't have done...."

She smacked him across the cheek.

"If you're Crow, he's your enemy as well as mine! He'd have killed me! He's an Ape!" She drew a long, shuddering breath. "And now we've got to move fast for your ship before the pack hunts us down."

"You make me sick!" He tried to pick up the revolver but could not bring himself to touch it.

"Keith, I'll make it up to you on the journey home, I promise. I ... I was desperate!"

"Just don't talk to me! Come on, let's git."

They slid past Arlblaster's body, out into the drizzling rain. As they started down the slope, a baying cry came from their left flank. A group of Neanderthals, men and women, stood on a promontory only two hundred yards away. They must have witnessed Arlblaster's collapse and were slowly marshaling their forces. As Alice and Anderson appeared, some of them ran forward.

"Run!" Alice shouted. "Down to the river! Swim it and we're safe."

Close together, they sped down the slippery incline where an imaginary glacier had flowed. Without a pause or word, they plunged through reeds and mud and dived fully dressed into the slow waters. Making good time, the Neanderthals rushed down the slope after them, but halted when they reached the river.

Gaining the far bank, Anderson turned and helped

Alice out of the water. She collapsed puffing on the grass.

"Not so young as I was.... We're safe now, Keith. Nothing short of a forest fire induces those apes to swim. But we still might meet trouble this side.... We'll avoid the settlement. Even if the apes there aren't after us, we don't want to face Stanley with his rifle.... Poor old Stanley! Give me a hand up."

Anderson moved on in surly silence. His mind was troubled by Arlblaster's death, and he felt he was being used.

The rain ceased as they pressed forward among dripping bushes. Traveling in a wide arc, they circled the village and picked up a track which led back toward Anderson's ship.

Alice grumbled intermittently as they went. At last Anderson turned on her.

"You don't have to come with me, Alice. If you want to, go back to Stanley Menderstone!"

"At least he cared about a woman's feelings."

"I warn you that they are not so fussy on Earth, where women don't have the same scarcity value." He hated himself for speaking so roughly. He needed solitude to sort out the turmoil in his brain.

Alice plodded along beside him without speaking. Sun gleamed. At last the black hull of the ship became visible between trees.

"You'll have to work on Earth!" he taunted her. "The robocracy will direct you."

"I'll get married. I've still got some looks."

"You've forgotten something, honey. Women have to have work certificates before they can marry these days. Regimentation will do you good."

A wave of hatred overcame him. He remembered the priestly Arlblaster dying. When Alice started to snap back at him, Anderson struck her on the shoulder. A look of panic and understanding passed over her face.

"Oh, Keith," she said, "you...." Her voice died; a change came over her face. He saw her despair before she turned and was running away, back toward the settlement, calling inarticulately as she ran.

Anderson watched her go. Then he turned and sidled through the dripping trees. At last—free! Himself! She was a Crow squaw.

His ship no longer looked welcoming. He splashed through a puddle and touched it, withdrawing his hand quickly. Distorted by the curve of the hull, his reflection peered at him from the polished metal. He did not recognize himself.

"Someone there imprisoned in Crow ship," he said, turning away.

The breath of the planet was warm along his innocent cheek. He stripped off his damp clothes and faded among the leaves and uncountable grasses and the scents of soil and vegetation. Shadow and light slithered over his skin in an almost tangible pattern before foliage embraced him and he was lost entirely into his new Eden.

The proud author lay where he was on the floor of the small room, among the metal sheets he had worn as camouflage while hiding with the humots. Since the Tenth Dominant finished reading his story—that poor thing written before he had wisdom—silence lay between the Dominant and the Chief Scanner; though whether or not they were communicating by UHF, Anderson could not tell.

He decided he had better do something. Sitting up, he said, "How about letting me go free? Or how about letting me go back to the zoo? ... Well, at least take me into a room that's big enough for me."

The Dominant spoke. "We need to ask you questions about your story. Is it true or not true?"

"It's fiction. Lousy or otherwise, it exists in its own right."

"Some things in it are true—you are. So is or was Frank Arlblaster. So is or was Stanley Menderstone. But other things are false. You did not stay always on Nehru II. You came back to Earth."

"The story is fiction. Forget it! It has nothing to do with you. Or with me, now. I only write poetry now—that story is just a thing I wrote to amuse myself."

"We do not understand it. You must explain it."

"Oh, Christ! ... Look, I wouldn't bother about it! I wrote it on the journey back to Earth from Nehru II, just to keep myself amused. When I got here, it was to find the various surviving Master Boffs were picking up such bits of civilization as were left around the world after Nuclear Week! The story immediately became irrelevant."

"We know all about Nuclear Week. We do not know about your story. We insist: we must know about it."

As Anderson sighed, he nevertheless recognized that more must lie in the balance here than he understood.

"I've been a bad boy, Dominant, I know. I escaped from the zoo. Put me back there, let me settle back with my wife; for my part, I'll not attempt to escape again. *Then* we'll talk about my story."

The silence lasted only a fraction of a second. "Done," said the Dominant, with splendid mastery of humanic idiom.

The zoo was not unpleasant. By current standards, it was vast, and the flats in the new human-type skyscrapers not too cramped; the liberals admitted that the Hive had been generous about space. There were about twenty thousand people here, the East Coast survivors of Nuclear Week. The robocracy had charge of them; they, in their turn, had charge of all the surviving wildlife that the automata could capture. Incongruous among the tall flat-blocks stood cages of exotic animals collected from shattered zoos—a pride of lions, some leopards, several cheetahs, an ocelot, camels. There were monkey houses, ostrich houses, elephant houses, aquaria, reptilia. There were pens full of pigs and sheep and cows. Exotic and native birds were captive in aviaries.

Keith Anderson sat on the balcony of his flat with his wife, Sheila, and drank an ersatz coffee, looking out onto the pens below, not without relish.

"Well, the robots are behaving very strangely," Sheila was saying. "When you disappeared, three of the very tiny ones came and searched everywhere. Your story was the only thing they seemed interested in. They must have photostated it."

"I remember now—it was in the trunk under the bed. I'd forgotten all about it till they mentioned it—my sole claim to literary fame!"

"But that side of it can't interest them. What are they excited about?"

He looked musingly at her. She was still partly a stranger to him, though a beloved one. In the chaos to which he returned after the Nehru trip, it was a case of marrying any eligible girl while they were available—men outnumbered women two to one; he'd been lucky in his blind choice. Sheila might not be particularly beautiful, but she was good in bed, trustworthy, and intelligent. You could ask for no more.

He said, "Do you ever admit the truth of the situation to yourself, Sheila? The new automata are now the superior race. They have a dozen faculties to each one of ours. They're virtually indestructible. Small size is clearly as much an enormous advantage to them as it would be a disadvantage to us. We've heard rumors that they were on the threshold of some staggering new discovery. From what I overheard the Tenth Dominant say, they are on the brink of moving into some staggering new dimensions of which we can probably never even get a glimpse. And yet. . . ."

"And yet they need your story!" She laughed—sympathetically, so that he laughed with her.

"Right! They need my goddamned story! Listen—their powers of planning and extrapolation are proved miraculous. But they cannot *imagine*; imagination might even be an impediment for them. So the Dominant, who can tap more knowledge than you or I dream of, is baffled by a work of fiction. He needs my imagination."

"Not entirely, Mr. Anderson."

Anderson jumped up, cup in hand, as his wife gave a small scream.

Perched on the balcony rail, enormously solid-looking, yet only six inches high, was the stubby shape of an automaton!

Furious, Anderson flung his cup, the only weapon to hand. It hit the machine squarely, shattered, and fell away. The machine did not even bother to refer to the matter.

"We understand imagination. We wish to ask you more questions about the background to your story."

Anderson sat down, took Sheila's hand, and made an anatomical suggestion which no automaton could have carried out.

"We want to ask you more questions about the story. Why did you write that you stayed on Nehru when really you came back?"

"Are you the Chief Scanner who captured me on D-Dump?"

"You are speaking with Tenth Dominant, in command of Eastern Seaboard. I have currently taken over Chief Scanner for convenience of speaking with you."

"Sort of mechanical transvestism, eh?"

"Why did you write that you stayed when you in reality came back?"

"You'd better give him straight answers, Keith," Sheila said.

He turned to her irritably, "How do I know the answer? It was just a story! I suppose it made a better ending to have the Anderson-figure stay on Nehru. There was this Cro-Magnon-Neanderthal business in the story and I made myself out to be more Neanderthal than Crow for dramatic effect. Just a lot of nonsense, really!"

"Why do you call it nonsense when you wrote it

yourself?" asked the Dominant. It had settled in the middle of the coffee table now.

The man sighed wearily. "Because I'm older now. The story was a lot of nonsense because I injected this Crow-Neanderthal theory, which is a bit of free-wheeling young man tripe. It just went in to try to explain what actually happened on Nehru—how the egghead camp broke down and everything. The theory doesn't hold water for a moment; I see that now, in the light of what happened since, Nuclear Week and all that. You see. . . ."

He stopped. He stopped in mid-sentence and stared at the little complex artifact confronting him. It was speaking to him, but he did not hear, following his own racing thoughts. He stretched forward his hand and picked it up; the automaton was heavy and warm, only mildly frightening, slightly, slightly vibrating at the power of its own voice; the Dominant did not stop him picking it up. He stared at it as if he had never seen such a thing before.

"I repeat, how would you revise your theory now?" said the automaton.

Anderson came back to reality.

"Why should I help you? To your kind, man is just another animal in a zoo, a lower species."

"Not so. We revere you as ancestors and have never treated you otherwise."

"Maybe. Perhaps we regard animals in somewhat the same way since, even in the darkest days of overpopulation and famine, we strove to stock our zoos in ever greater numbers. So perhaps I will tell you my current theory. . . . It is real theory now; in my story that theory was not worth the name—it was a stunt, an intellectual high-jinks, a bit of science fiction. Now I have lived and thought and loved and suffered, and I have talked to other men. So if I tell you the theory now, you will know it is worked for—part of the heritage of all men in this zoo."

"This time it is truth not false?"

"You are the boss—*you* must decide that. There are certainly two distinct parts of the brain, the old limbic section and the neocortex surrounding it, the bit that turns a primate into a man. That much of my story was true. There's also a yet older section, but we won't complicate the picture. Roughly speaking, the limbic is the seat of the emotions, and the neocortex the seat of the intelligence. Okay. In a crisis, the new brain is still apt to cut out and the old brain take over.

"And that in a nutshell is why mankind never made the grade. We are a failed species. We never got away from the old animal inheritance. We could never become the distinct species we should have been."

"Oh, darling, it's not as bad as that. . . ."

He squeezed Sheila's hand. "You girls are always optimists." He winked the eye the Dominant could not see.

The Dominant said, "How does this apply to what happened on Nehru II?"

"My story departed—not from the facts—but from the correct explanation of the facts. The instinct to go there on Swettenham's part was sound. He and Arlblaster and the rest believed that on a planet away from animals, mankind could achieve its true stature—homo superior, shall we say? What I called the N-factor let them down. The strain was too great, and they mainly reverted instead of evolving."

"But you believe a species can only escape its origins by removing itself entirely from the site of those origins."

Sheila said, "That was the whole human impulse behind space travel—to get to worlds where it would be possible to become more human."

The Dominant sprang from Anderson's hands and circled under the low ceiling—an oddly uneasy gesture.

"But the limbic brain—such a small part of the brain, so deep-buried!"

"The seat of the instincts."

"The seat of the instincts. . . . Yes, and so the animal part of man brought you to disaster."

"Does that answer all your questions?"

The automaton came back down and settled on the table. "One further question. What do you imagine would happen to mankind now, after Nuclear Week, if he was left alone on Earth?"

Anderson had to bury his face in his hands to hide his triumph.

"I guess we'd carry on. Under D-Dump, and the other dumps, lie many of the old artifacts. We'd dig them up and carry on."

"But Earth's resources are almost spent. That was mankind's doing, not the doing of automata."

The man smiled. "Maybe we'd revert, then. It is a sort of Neanderthal planet, isn't it? Things go wrong for animals and men and robots, don't they? Just as they did for dinosaurs and Neanderthals!"

"I am going now," said the Tenth Dominant. His voice cut. He disappeared.

Gasping, Anderson clutched his wife. "Don't say a word! Come inside. Hold me and kiss me. Pray, if you feel like it."

All she said as they went to their bed was, "Maybe you will end up a writer after all. You show a talent for storytelling!"

It was all of five days before the human beings in the big zoo noticed that the automata were disappearing. Suddenly, they were all gone, leaving no word. The whole continent, presumably the whole world, lay almost empty; and mankind began to walk back into it on his own ill-shod feet.

"And you did it, Keith Anderson!" Sheila cried.

"Nope. They did it themselves. They made the right decision—maybe I spurred them on."

"You did it—a genius who is now going to turn himself into a pig-breeder."

"I happen to like pigs." As he spoke, he stood in the middle of a dozen of the animals, which he and Sheila had taken charge of.

"So the entire automata horde has disappeared into the invospectrum, wherever that is, leaving us our world...."

"It's a different world. Let's try and make it saner than the old one."

Pious hope? New Year's resolution? New design for living? He could not tell, although it filled his mind.

As they drove the pigs before them, Anderson said, "When the Dominant got onto the subject of our animal inheritance, I remembered just in time that I heard him tell the Scanner, 'We must free ourselves from our human heritage.' You can see the spot they were in! They had scrapped the humots, all too clearly anthropomorphic in design, and had taken more functional forms themselves. But they still had to acknowledge us as father-figures and could never escape from many human and naturalistic concepts, however much they tried, as long as they remained in a naturalistic setting. Now, in this unimaginable alternative-energy universe, which they have finally cracked, they can be pure automata—which is something else we can't conceive! So they become a genuine species. Pure automata...."

They broke off to drive their pigs through the doorway, doubling back and forth until all the animals were inside, squealing and trying to leap over one another's backs. Anderson slammed the outer door at once, gasping.

"What I'd like to know is, what would it be like to be pure human being!" Sheila exclaimed.

He had no answer. He was thinking. Of course, they needed a dog! On D-Dump there were feral hounds whose young could be caught and trained.

It was lucky that the ground-floor tenants had gone. Most human beings had moved out of the zoo as soon as possible, so that the great block of flats was almost empty. They shut the pigs in the hall for the night and climbed up rather wearily to their flat.

Today, they were too tired to bother about the future.

Danger: Religion!

We made a strange group, the four of us plodding manfully through nowhere.

Royal Meacher, my brother, led the way. His long arms and bony hands fought the wind for possession of his cloak, a shabby mantle that stayed about him no more certainly than his authority.

Next, the breeze from the north plucked at the figure of Turton, our man Turton, poor old Turton, the mutant whose third arm and all but useless third leg combined with his black cloak to give him from behind something of the appearance of a beetle. Over his shoulder, Turton carried Candida in an attitude of maximum discomfort.

Candida still dripped. Her hair streamed in the wind like frayed ribbon. Her left ear jogged up and down the central seam of Turton's coat; her right eye peered sightlessly back at me. Candida is Royal's fourth wife.

I am Royal's younger brother, Sheridan. I felt defeated by Candida's stare. I kept hoping that the jig-jog of Turton's walk would shake her eye shut; and so I suppose it might have done had her head not been hanging upside down.

We walked toward the north, into the molars of the wind.

The road on which we walked was narrow and absolutely straight. It appeared to lead nowhere, for despite the wind a miasmal mist rose from the damp about us, obscuring everything ahead. The road ran along a dyke, the sides of which, being newly constructed, were of bare earth. This dyke divided a stretch of sea. We had the sea on both sides of us.

Almost as far as our vision extended, we could see another dyke extending parallel with ours. The sea was being chopped into polders. In time, as the work of reclamation proceeded, the squares would be drained; the sea would dwindle into puddles; the puddles would become mud; the mud would become soil; the soils would become vegetables; and the vegetables—oh, yes!—the vegetables would be eaten and become flesh; ghosts of future people grew here.

Treading steadily on to the rear of Turton, I looked back over my shoulder.

The vast funeral pyre we had left was made insignificant by distance; the kiln was a tiny black pipe topped by flame. No more did we feel its heat or smell the burning bodies, but the effluvium lingered in our memories. Royal still spoke of it, rambling in and out of quotation as his habit was, addressing the wind.

"You note how the parsimonious Dutch reclaim both their land and their dead in one operation. And those grisly corpses, maligned by sea and radiation, will make excellent fertilizer with their ashes. How convenient, how concise! Occam's razor cuts precious fine, friends: the obscene fag ends of one chemical reaction go to start another. 'Marvellous is the plan by which this best of worlds is wisely planned!' Forty thousand dead Dutchmen should guarantee us a good cabbage crop in four years, eh, Turton?"

The bent old man, with Candida's head nodding idiot agreement, said, "Back before the last two wars, they used to grow tulips and flowers here, according to the engineer at the kiln."

Dark was coming in now, the mist thickening, the sulky captive sea falling motionless as the wind died. Beyond the outline of my brother's back I could see

lights; with gratitude I mouthed their ugly name;
Noordoostburg-op-Langedijk.

"That moldy towerful of cadavers would seem to
be less appropriately applied to tulips than to cabbages, Turton," Royal said. "And what more suitable
envoi to the indignity of their deaths? Recollect your
Browne: 'To be gnawed out of our graves, to have our
skulls made drinking bowls, and our bones turned
into pipes, to delight and sport our enemies—'how
does it go?'—are tragical abominations escaped in
burning burials.' Since Browne's time, we've grown a
lot more ingenious! Nuclear destruction and incineration need not be the end of our troubles. We can
still be spread as mulch for the genus brassica. . . ."

"Cabbages it was, cabbages or tulips," old Turton
insisted, but Royal was not to be deflected. He talked
on as we trudged on. I was not listening. I wanted
only to get off this eternal earthwork, safe into civilization and warmth.

When we reached Noordoostburg-op-Langedijk, a
mere platform joined by dyke and mole to the distant
land, we went into its only café. Turton laid Candida
down on a bench. He unbent his beetle back and
stretched his arms (but the third never stretched
straight) with groans of relief. The café manager
came forward hurriedly.

"I regret I cannot introduce you properly to my
wife. She is religious and has passed into a coma,"
Royal said, staring the man down.

"Sir, this lady is not dead?" the manager asked.

"Merely religious."

"Sir, she is somewhat wet!" the manager said.

"A property she shares with the confounded ditch
into which she plunged when the coma overtook her,
my man. Will you kindly bring us three soups: my
wife, as you see, will not partake."

Dubiously the manager backed away.

Turton followed him to the counter.

"You see, the lady's very susceptible to anything religious. We came over with the party from Edinburgh specially to see the cremation down the road, and Mrs. Meacher was overwhelmed by the sight. Or perhaps it was the smell, I don't know, or the sound of the bodies bubbling in the incinerator. Anyhow, before anyone could stop her, backward she went—splash!—and—"

"Turton!" Royal called sharply.

"I was just trying to borrow a towel," Turton said.

We ate our soup in silence. A puddle collected under Candida's clothing.

"Say something, Sheridan," Roy demanded, rapping his spoon on the table at me.

"I wonder if there are fish in those fields," I said.

He made his usual gesture of disgust and turned away. Fortunately I did not have to say anything more, for at that moment the rest of our Edinburgh party came in for soup. The incineration ceremony had finished just after we left.

Soup and rationed chocolate were all that the café offered. When the party had finished up their bowls, we went outside. I draped Candida over Turton's shoulder, and we followed Royal.

The weather was showing its talents. The wind had dropped; rain began to fall. It fell on the concrete, into the polders, into the sour sea. It fell onto the buzz-jet. We all packed into it, jostling and pushing. Somehow, Royal managed to get in and away from the rain first. Turton and I were last aboard, but Turton had been wet already.

This buzz-jet was a missile left over from the last war and converted. It was uncomfortable, yet it could move; we headed northwest across the sea and over northern England, where not a light showed from the stricken lands; in a quarter of an hour the lights of Edinburgh showed through the slashing darkness.

Our craft was a government one. Private transport of any variety was a thing of the past. Mainly it was fuel shortage that had brought the situation about;

but when the last war ended at the beginning of 2041, the government passed laws forbidding the private ownership of transport.

At Turnhouse Airport we climbed out and made our way with the crowd to a bus shelter. A bus arrived after a few minutes; it was too full to take us; we waited and caught the next one; it crawled with us into town, while we stood like cattle in a truck.

That sort of thing takes the edge off what otherwise had been a very enjoyable day's sightseeing. We had made several such excursions to celebrate my demobilization from the army.

Since the war, Edinburgh had become the capital of Europe, chiefly because the others had been obliterated or made uninhabitable by radiation or the aftereffects of bacterial warfare.

Some of the old Scottish families were proud of this promotion of their city; others felt that this greatness had been thrust upon them; but most of them took advantage of the shining hour by thrusting up rents to astronomical heights. The thousands of refugees, evacuated and displaced people who poured into the city, found themselves held to ransom for living space.

When we climbed out of the bus at the city center, I became separated from the others by the crowd, that cursed anonymous crowd speaking all the tongues of Europe. I brushed off a hand that clutched at my sleeve; it came again, detaining me more forcibly. Irritably, I looked round, and my eyes met the eyes of a square, dark man; in that instance, I took in no more detail beyond saying to myself that his was a great Gothic cathedral of a face.

"You are Sheridan Meacher, fellow of Edinburgh University, lecturer in history?" he asked.

I dislike being recognized at a bus stop.

"European history," I said.

The expression on his face was not readable; weary triumph, perhaps? He motioned to me to follow him.

At that moment, the crowd surged forward, so that he and I were borne out of it and into a side street.

"I want you to come with me," he said.

"Who are you? I've got no money."

He wore a black and white uniform. That did not endear him to me. I had seen enough of uniforms in those weary war years underground.

"Mr. Meacher, you are in trouble. I have a room not five minutes away from here; will you please come with me to it and discuss the situation with me? I assure you I will offer you no personal harm, if that is why you hesitate."

"What sort of trouble? Are you a black marketeer? If so, shove off!"

"Let us go and discuss."

I shrugged my shoulders and followed him. We went down a couple of back streets, toward the Grassmarket, and in at a grimy door. The man with the Gothic face preceded me up a winding stair. At one point a door opened, a dimly lit hag's face peeped out at us, and then the door slammed again, leaving us in gloom.

He paused on a landing and felt in his pocket. He said, "I shouldn't think a house like this has changed much since Dr. Johnson visited Edinburgh." Then in an altered tone, he added, "I mean—you did have a Dr. Johnson, Samuel Johnson—didn't you?"

Not understanding his phrasing—yet I had not taken him for other than an Englishman—I said, "Dr. Johnson visited this city to stay with his friend Boswell about 1773 A.D.

In the dark he sighed with relief. Sliding a key into a lock he said, "Of course, of course, I was just forgetting that the road from London to Edinburgh was open by that date. Forgive me."

He opened a door, switched on a light, and ushered me into his room. What could the man mean? Edinburgh and London had been connected—though often tenuously—a long while before Johnson's visit. I was beginning to form ideas about this Gothic stranger—all of them later proved wrong.

His room was bare and nondescript, a typical lodging room with a combo-toilet in one corner, in another a hand generator in case the main electricity supply failed, and a screen standing on the far side of the room with a bed behind it. He went across to the window to draw the curtains before turning to confront me.

"I should introduce myself, Mr. Meacher. My name is Apostolic Rastell, Captain Apostolic Rastell of the Matrix Investigation Corps."

I inclined my head and waited; the world was full of sinister-sounding establishments these days, and although I had never heard of the Matrix Investigation Corps, I did not say so. We stood looking at each other, summing one another up. Captain Rastell was a considerable man, untidy perhaps, but prepossessing, strongly built without being bulky, a man in his late twenties, and with that square, dogged, extraordinary face. I could not make him out—truth to tell, I have never been able to make him out.

He went behind his screen, to emerge carrying a light folding screen. This he opened and stood up.

The screen was locked with some sort of a combination lock. Rastell worked it, staring at me somewhat grimly as he listened to the tumblers click.

"You had better look at this before I offer any explanation," he said.

A seat unfolded from the screen, and behind it, the screen surface turned silver and mirrorlike. I took a good look, and faintness overcame me. I staggered and he caught me, but I quickly recovered.

I saw myself in the screen. The anonymous room was also reflected there, if reflected is the word, its dimensions cramped and twisted, so that it looked as if the figures of Rastell and myself stood on the outside rather than the inside of a cube. The effect was as if I peered into a distorting mirror; but this was no mirror—for I found myself staring distractedly at my own profile!

"What's this bit of gimmickry?"

"You are an intelligent man, Mr. Meacher, and since I am in a hurry I hope that already this sight has suggested to you that there are departments of life which are a mystery to you, and into which you have not peered or cared to peer. There are other earths, other Edinburghs, than this one of yours, Mr. Meacher; I come from such a one, and I invite you to follow me back to it now."

I sat on a chair and stared at him. There is no point in recounting the terrors, hopes, and suppositions that poured through my mind. After a moment, I listened to what he was saying. It went something like this:

"Although you are not a philosopher, Mr. Meacher, you perhaps understand how many men spend large parts of their lives waiting for a challenge; they prepare themselves for it, though they may not guess what it is until the moment comes. I hope you are such a man, for I have no time for lengthy explanation. In the matrix from which I came, we had a dramatist last century called Jean Paul Sartre; in one of his plays, a man says to another, 'Do you mean to say that you would judge the whole of someone's life by one single action?' and the other asks simply, 'Why not?' So I ask you, Mr. Meacher, will you come with me? Will you test all your life with one action?"

"Why should I?"

"*You* must ask *yourself* that." In the circumstances, what monstrous assumptions behind that remark!

"You will come? Excellent!" he said, moving forward and grasping my arm. Unthinkingly, I had risen, and he had taken my rising for assent. Perhaps it was.

I allowed myself to be led over to the seat in his—let me use his own term—his "portal." He saw me settled there and said, "This is nothing that you are unprepared for; you may be astonished, but you are not surprised. It will be news for you, but probably

nothing upon which you have not privately specu-
lated, when I tell you that the earth you know is
merely a three-dimensional appearance—an outcrop,
a geologist would call it—of a multidimensional universe. To comprehend the total multidimensional universe is beyond man's power and perhaps always will
be, one impediment being that his senses register
each of its dimensions as a three-dimensional reality."

"Rastell, for God's sake, I don't know what you are
saying!"

"The violence of your denial persuades me otherwise. Let me put it this way, with an analogy with
which you may be familiar.

"A two-dimensional creature lives on a sheet of
paper. A bubble—that is, a three-dimensional object—
passes through the paper. How does the two-
dimensional creature perceive the bubble? First as a
point, which expands to a circle that at its maximum
is the circumference of the bubble; the bubble is then
halfway through paper; the circle then begins to con-
tract until it becomes a point and disappears in the
next instant."

"Yes, yes, I understand all that, but are you trying
to imply that this two-dimensional creature can climb
onto the bubble, which is. . . ."

"Listen, all that stops the creature climbing onto
the bubble is its attitude of mind, its system of logic.
Its mind needs a twist through ninety degrees—and
so does yours. Join the creature's strip of paper up at
both ends and you get a lively representation of your
mind; a closed circle! You can't perceive the other
matrices of the multidimensional universe. But I can
make you perceive them. I'm going to give you an
injection now, Mr. Meacher, that will have that effect
on your perceptions."

It was crazy! He must somehow have hypnotized
me—fascinated me certainly!—to make me go as far
as that with him. I jumped up from the chair.

"Leave me alone, Rastell! I don't know what you

are saying, and I don't want to. I don't want any part of it. I lost my sense of adventure in the army. I—Rastell!"

His name came from my lips as a shriek. He had put out a hand as if to steady me, and plunged the tip of a small hypodermic into the vein of my left wrist. A stinging sensation coursed up my arm.

As I swung toward him, I brought my right fist up, aiming a blow at his face. He ducked, and, carried off balance, I staggered forward.

"I'd sit down if I were you, Meacher. You have nicomiotine in your veins, and, if you are unused to it, exertion may make you sick. Sit down, man."

My gaze fixed on his face, with its tall lines, and the extraordinarily sensible relationship between its various features. I saw that face, graven onto my sight, as a central point, a cardinal fact, a reference from which the whole universe might be mapped; for the influence of time and event lay in that face, until it in its time influenced time and event, and in that linkage I saw symbolized the whole wheel of life that governs men. Yes, I knew—even at that time I knew— that already I was gliding under the influence of the drug Rastell had given me. It made no difference. Truth is truth, whether you find it or it finds you.

When I sat down in the seat, it was with a motion that held the same magic dualism. For the act might have looked like submission to another's will; yet I knew it was more vitally a demonstration of *my* will, as inside the universe of my body a part of me had brought into play a thousand minute responses, and blood and muscle cooperated in the act. At the same time that this dramatic and cosmic act was in process, I was hearing the voice of Rastell, booming at me from a distance.

"In this matrix of yours, I understand you passed through what is now referred to as the Tobacco Age, when many people—this applied particularly to the first half of the last century—were slaves to the tobacco habit. It was the age of the cigarette. Cigarettes were not the romantic objects portrayed by our historical novelists; they were killers, for the nicotine contained in them, though beneficial to the brain in small quantities, is death to the lungs when scattered over them in large quantities. However, before the cigarette finally went out of production toward the end of the seventies—how are you feeling, Meacher? It won't take long—before the downfall of the cigarette firms, they developed nicomiotine. Because the firms were in general bad repute, the new drug lay neglected for fifty years; in this matrix of yours, it is neglected still, as far as I can ascertain."

He felt my pulse, which labored beneath my skin like a man struggling to free himself from imprisonment in a sack. Sunk in an ocean of feeling, I said nothing; I could see the benefit of remaining unconscious all one's life. Then one could be free to pursue the real things.

"You probably won't know this, Meacher, but nicotine used to retard the passing of urine. It set in motion a chain of reactions which released a substance called vasopressin from the pituitary gland into the bloodstream; when the vasopressin reached the kidney, the excretion of water taken by the mouth was suppressed.

"Nicomiotine releases noradrenaline from the hypothalamus and from the tegmentum of the limbic brain, that part of the brain which controls the functions of consciousness. At the same time, the drug builds up miodrenaline in the peripheral blood vessels. This results in what we call an 'attention transfer.' The result—I'm simplifying here, Meacher—the result is the dislocation of consciousness necessary for switching over from one matrix to another. The flow of attention is, so to speak, given a Mobius twist and tagged onto the next matrix."

"Curiouser and curiouser," I murmured.

"The seat on which you sit is in a circuit which can

be turned to various vibratory levels, each of which corresponds to one matrix of the multidimensional universe. I move this switch here, and you will slip easily through the portal into the matrix from which I have come. Don't think of it as going through a barrier; rather, you are avoiding a barrier.

"The effects of this technique can also be achieved by long mental discipline; it was this that the yogi were unwittingly reaching out for when they—ah, you are sliding through now, Meacher. Don't be alarmed."

I was not alarmed. I was standing outside my own shell and seeing that to all of us come moments of calm and detachment; that stillness might be the secret which only a handful of men in any generation stumbles on. In the same long-drawn moment of time, I was aware that my left foot had disintegrated.

No dismay assailed me, for the right foot had disintegrated too. The wisdom and symmetry of this event pleased me.

Everything was disintegrating into mist—not that I took it seriously, although for a moment I was frightened by the basilisk stare of my jacket buttons, glaring up unwinkingly at me, so that I was reminded of those lines of Rimbaud's about "the coat buttons that are eyes of wild creatures glaring at you from the end of the corridors." Then buttons and Rimbaud and I were gone into mist!

A feeling of sickness preceded me into Rastell's matrix.

I sat up shivering in the seat, my head suddenly clear and my body temperature low. The drug had built up a certain pitch and then abandoned me. It was as if a passionate love affair had been ended by an unexpected desertion, a betraying letter. In my misery, I looked about me and saw a room very like the room I had left.

The room was the same shape; it had the same doors and windows, with the same view out of the window; but the curtains were not drawn, and it was light outside. I fancied the furniture was different, but had not taken in the other room clearly enough to be positive. One thing I was sure of: the other room had not contained a little ugly man dressed in overalls standing motionless by the door, staring at me.

As I got to my feet, Rastell materialized, pulling the collapsible screen with him.

"You'll soon feel better," he said. "The first time's always the worst. Now we'll have to get a move on. Can you walk all right? We'll catch a cab in the street."

"Where are we, Rastell? This is still Edinburgh. What's happened? If you are fooling with me...."

He snapped his fingers impatiently but answered in a quiet voice.

"You have left the Edinburgh of AA688, which is how we designate your home matrix. We are now in the Edinburgh of AA541. In many respects, one much resembles the other. In some ways you will find them identical. Only the workings of chance have brought divergencies from what you at first will think of as the norm. As you adjust to inter-matrix living, you'll realize that norms do not exist. Let's move."

"I don't understand what you are saying. Are you saying that I may find my brother and his wife here?"

"Why not? It's quite possible that you may find yourself here—here and in a thousand other matrices. It is a property of matter to imitate itself in all matrices and of chance to modify the imitations."

He said this as if repeating some sort of received idea, walking over as he did to the shabby fellow, who, all this time, had stood patiently unmoving by the door. I saw this fellow wore a bracelet over his overalls below one knee; from the bracelet radiated four short arms that bit into his flesh. Rastell produced a key from his pocket and thrust it into a lock in the bracelet. The four arms fell outward and hung loosely from their hinges on the bracelet's rim. The man rubbed his leg and hobbled around the room, restoring his circulation. He kept his eye on both Rastell and me, but especially on me, without looking at either of us directly, and without speaking.

"Who is this man? What are you doing?" I asked.

"He would have tried to escape while I was away if I had not locked him still," Rastell said. He produced a bottle from under his tunic. "They still have whiskey in this matrix, Meacher, you'll be glad to hear. Have a good pull—it will help you take control of yourself."

Gratefully, I drank the warming stuff from the bottle.

"I'm in control of myself, Rastell. But this talk of matter imitating itself in all matrices—it's like a vision of hell. For God's sake, how many matrices are there?"

"There is not time to go into all that now. You shall have the answers if you help us. As yet, in any case, we have uncovered more questions than answers. Verification of the existence of the multimatrix universe came no more than twenty years ago; the Matrix Investigation Corps was established only fifteen years ago, in 2027, the year the Fourth World War broke out in your matrix. In this matrix, the war did not take place."

"Rastell, I cannot accept a word you are saying. I want no part of this."

"You are a part of it. Dibbs, get the portal folded up."

Dibbs was the voiceless one. Keeping his eyes to the ground, he did as he was told, folding the portal to the size of a satchel and clipping it onto Rastell's back. Rastell grabbed my arm and pulled me around, not unkindly.

"Pull yourself together and let's get along. I know it's a shock at first, but you are a man of intelligence; you'll adjust."

I knocked his hand away.

"It's because I'm a man of intelligence that I reject all this. How many of these matrix worlds are there?"

"The Matrix Investigation Corps measures consciousness in dees. Spaced three dees apart from each other lies an infinity of matrices—yes, an infinity, Meacher, and I see the word does little to reassure you. Only a few dozen worlds are explored as yet. One or two we are using. Some are so nearly identical to ours that only by a few details—the taste maybe of the whiskey or the name of a Sunday newspaper—do they differ at all; others—we found one, Meacher, where the earth was in an improperly created state, just a ball of turbulent rivers of mud, lying under permanent cloud. On one, there were only winged things in a forest world."

He opened the door as he was speaking, and we went together down the winding stair and out into the street by a grimy door.

My adventure had begun. At the sight of that grimy alien door opening, I was myself again, excited by the challenging novelty of everything.

It had been evening when I went into that house, or a house like it. Now it was iron-gray day, with a daylight forged to match the stones of the city. Oh yes, this was Auld Reekie all right, unmistakably Auld Reekie—and unmistakably not the Edinburgh I had been born in.

True, the buildings looked similar, though a strangeness in the pattern they presented told me that some of them were altered in ways I did not recollect. The people looked different and dressed differently.

Gone were the shabby and talkative crowds among which Royal, Candida, and I had jostled only a short while before. The streets were almost empty, and those that moved about on them were easily observed to fall into two classes. Some men and women there were who traveled the streets with their heads held high, who walked briskly, who smiled and saluted each other; they were well dressed, in what I thought of then as a "futuristic" style, with wide plain collars and short cloaks of what looked like a stiff leather or plastic. Many of the men wore swords. This class of people walked on the sidewalks.

There was another class of people. These men were allowed to use only the road itself for walking. They did not greet each other; they moved through the streets with no grace in their carriage, for whether they walked or loped—as many of them did—they kept their heads down and looked about furtively from under their brows. Like Dibbs, they all wore overalls, like him they carried spiked bracelets below one knee, and like him they bore a yellow disc on their backs, between their shoulder blades.

I had plenty of time to observe these people, for Rastell, as he had promised, had got us a cab, and in this we set off in the direction of Waverley Station.

The cab amazed me. It was worked by manpower. Three men in overalls—I was already, I think, referring to them mentally as the slave class—were chained to a seat behind the cab; Dibbs climbed up with them to make a fourth; together they worked away at foot pedals, and that was the way we moved, propelled by four sweating wretches.

In the streets, several similar cabs were bowling along, and there were even sedan chairs, well suited to the uneven nature of Edinburgh's topography. There were also men riding horseback and occasional conventional trucks with internal-combustion engines. I saw no buses or private cars. Remembering how the latter class of vehicle had been forbidden in my own matrix, I asked Rastell about it.

"We happen to have more manpower than we have fuels," he said. "And unlike your wretchedly proletarian matrix, here most free men have leisure and find no need to hurry everywhere."

"You impressed on me the need for hurry."

"We are hurrying because the balance of this entire

matrix is in a state of crisis. Civilization is threatened and must be saved. You and others like you from other matrices are being brought here because we need the perspective that an extra-matricial can give. Because your culture is inferior to ours does not mean that your abilities may not be invaluable.

"Inferior? What do you mean, inferior? You appear to be a couple of centuries behind us, with your antiquated sedans and these anachronistic pedal cabs."

"You don't measure progress just by materialistic standards, Meacher, I hope?" Up came his Gothic eyebrows as he spoke.

"Indeed I don't. I measure it by personal liberty, and from the bare glimpse I have had of your culture—your matrix—you live in nothing better than a slave state."

"There is nothing better than a slave state. You are a historian, aren't you, a man capable of judging not simply by the parochial standards of his own time? What race became great without slave labor, including the Soviet Union and the British Empire? Was not Classical Greece a community of slave states? Who but slaves left all the lasting monuments of the world? In any case, you are prejudging. We have here a subject population, which is a different thing from slavery."

"Is it different for the people concerned?"

"Oh, for Church's sake, be silent, Meacher. You do nothing but verbalize."

"Why invoke the church about it?"

"Because I am a member of the Church. Take care not to blaspheme, Meacher. During your stay here, you will naturally be subject to our laws, and the Church keeps a firmer hold over its rights than it does in your matrix."

I fell gloomily silent. We had labored up onto George IV Bridge. Two of the slaves, working at the farthest extent of their chains, had jumped down from the back of the cab and pushed us over that stretch of the way. Having crossed the bridge, we began to go steeply down by The Mound, braking and freewheeling alternately, though a flywheel removed most of the unpleasant jerkiness from this method of progress. Edinburgh Castle, grandly high on our left, looked unchanged to me, but in the more modern part of the town before us I saw much change, without being able to identify any particular bit of it with certainty; for Royal, Candida, and I had not lived very long in Edinburgh, and we were not completely familiar with it.

Whistles sounded ahead. I took no notice, until Rastell stiffened and drew a revolver from his pocket. Ahead, by the steps of the Assembly Hall, a cab had crashed and turned over on its side. The three slaves attached to it could be seen—we had them in sight just around the bend—wrenching at their chains, trying to detach them from the cab. A passenger had survived the crash. He had his head out of the window and was blowing a whistle.

"The subs have allowed another crash—this is their favorite spot," Rastell said. "They get too negligent."

"It's a difficult corner. How can you tell they allowed it to happen?"

Giving me no answer, Rastell half opened the door of our cab and leaned out to shout at our slaves.

"Hey, you subs, stop this cab at once. I want to get out. Dibbs, jump down!"

We squealed to a halt on the slope. When Rastell jumped out I did the same. The air was cold. I was stiff and uneasy, well aware that I was so far from home that the distance could not be measured in miles. I looked about, and Dibbs and the three peddlers watched me with their eyebrows.

"Better follow me, Meacher," Rastell called. He broke into a run toward the wrecked cab. One of the slaves there had wrenched his chain from its anchorage in the wooden panels of the cab. Moving forward, he swung the loose end of the chain and brought it across the head of the passenger. The whistling stopped in mid-note. The passenger sagged to one side and then slid out of sight into the cab. By that time, the slave had jumped onto the top of the cab and turned to face Rastell. Other whistles began to shrill. A siren wailed.

When the slave on the cab saw that Rastell carried a gun, his expression changed. I saw his look of dismay as he motioned his fellows who were still captive and jumped down behind the cab. His fellows stood there trembling, no longer trying to get away.

Rastell did not fire. A car came tearing up the hill with sirens wailing and bucked to a halt between Rastell and the upturned cab. On the roof of the car was a winking sign that read CHURCH POLICE. Black-and-white-uniformed men jumped out. They wore swords and carried guns. Rastell hurried over to them.

I stayed where I was, half in the shelter of our cab, undecided, not wanting any part of anything. Dibbs and his fellow subs stood where they were, not moving, not speaking.

A crowd was collecting by the steps of the Assembly Hall, a crowd composed of the ruling class. The sub who had broken loose was kicked into the back of a police car. While the others indulged in argument, I had time to look at the police car more carefully. It was an odd vehicle, driven by an internal-combustion engine, a powerful beast, but without any of the streamlining characteristic of the cars with which I grew up. It had a double door set in either side, and another, through which the wretched sub was pushed, at the back. Its windows were narrow, pointed, and grouped in pairs, in the style of windows in Early English churches; even the windshield had been divided into six in this way. The whole thing was elaborately painted in white and light blue and yellow. Why not, I thought, if you have plenty of time and slave labor is cheap?

And the stained-glass motif about the windshield—why not, if most of the people you are likely to knock down are expendable and have no rights?

Rastell was returning, though the debate around the steps of the Assembly Hall was still in progress.

"Let's get on," Rastell said. He signaled curtly to Dibbs and the subs. We all climbed aboard and resumed our journey. I looked at the crowd about the church police car as we passed it. With a start, I thought I recognized one of the hangers-on in the crowd. He looked much like my brother Royal; then I told myself that my nerves were being irresponsible.

"There's too much of that sort of incident," Rastell said. "This trouble flared up all at once a few years ago. They must have a leader."

"I'd guess they also had a cause. What will happen to the man who broke free from the cab and clubbed the passenger?"

"That sub?" He looked at me, his lips curving in a smile not entirely free from malice. "He struck a churchgoer. I was not the only witness. He'll be hanged at the castle next week. What else could we do with him? He'll be granted last rites."

The grand stretch of Princes Street, a street fit for any capital, was changed, although many buildings were as I knew them. Their rather commercial gaiety had gone. They presented a drab uniformity now. Their windows were unwashed; the goods displayed for sale in the shop windows looked uninviting. I peered eagerly at them as we thudded by at a stiff walking pace. The big electronic showrooms had gone, the shops were not piled with the gadgets I knew.

On the sidewalks, greater variety was in evidence. Many people were about, looking cheerful as they shopped. Few slaves were in sight, and I now observed that among the free some were evidently far less prosperous than others. Sedans, pedal cabs, four-wheel bicycles, and little electrically powered cars moved busily about. I was sorry when we halted before a large gray building and Rastell signaled me to alight.

"This is the headquarters of my chapter," he said, as we pushed through the door with Dibbs following.

"I believe it's a block of offices in my matrix."

"On the contrary, it is the Commission for Nuclear Rearmament. Are you already forgetting how war oriented your matrix is?" He relented then and said, in less ironic tones, "However, you'll probably find us too religious. It's a matter of viewpoint, really."

The place was bustling. The foyer reminded me of an old-fashioned hotel; its furniture was cumbersome and oddly designed, reminding me of the late Windsor style of fifty years ago or more, except that everything was so colorless.

Rastell marched over to a bulletin board and scanned it.

"We have half an hour before the next history briefing for extra-matricials. You'd better attend; the less time wasted the better. I'll see you are found a room where you can wash and rest. I have one or two people I ought to speak to. We'll meet again, shortly, at the briefing."

A sub ran up to unclip the portal from his back. Another ran up with a glass of water. Captain Apostolic Rastell looked pleased to be home.

He signaled a passing servant, a girl dressed not in overalls but in a curious black and white pantaloon. I felt some anxiety at leaving Rastell, this one contact with my own matrix. He interpreted my expression and nodded at the girl.

"This sub girl will take good care of you, Meacher. Under the dispensation, she will serve you in any way you may require."

As he disappeared, I thought he was not an unlikable devil, given better circumstances. I followed the sub girl, noting the yellow disc between her shoulder blades. She led me up one flight of stairs and along a corridor and opened a door for me. When I was inside, she followed, locked the door, and handed me the key. Despite myself, her air of submissiveness gave me ideas. In that awful dress she looked foolish, and her face was pasty, but she was young and had good features.

"What's your name?"

She pointed to a button on her dress. On it was stamped the name Ann.

"You are Ann? Can't you talk?"

She shook her head. Cold needles prickled in my chest; it occurred to me that I had not heard a word from Dibbs or from the slaves by the upturned cab. Moving toward her, I touched her chin.

"Open your mouth, Ann."

Meekly, she let her jaw hang. No, her tongue was there, as well as several teeth that needed stopping or pulling. The helplessness of the creature overwhelmed me.

"Why can't you speak, Ann?"

She closed her jaw and lifted up her chin. On the whiteness of her neck ran an ugly scar. They had severed her vocal cords. I clasped her thin shoulders and let anger burn over me.

"Is this done to all slaves?"

Shake of head.

"To some—to most of them?"

Nod.

"Some sort of punishment?"

Nod.

"Hurt you?"

Nod. So remote!

"Are there other men like me, from other matrices, along this corridor?"

Blank look.

"I mean, other strangers from other places like me?"

Nod.

"Take me to one of them."

I gave her back the key. She unlocked the door and went into the corridor. At the door of the room next to mine she stopped. Her key fitted that lock, and the door swung open.

A fellow with a thatch of wispy yellow hair and stubble all around a great jaw sat at a table eating. He ate with a spoon, furiously. Though he looked up as I came in, pulling Ann in with me, he did not interrupt the ladling of food into his mouth.

"You're an extra-matricial?" I asked. He made noises of assent into his stew.

"So am I. The name's Sheridan Meacher. Historian, ex-army." When he made no answer save to gape, I went on. "We can't agree to give these people any help to bolster up their regime. Their entire system is evil and must be destroyed. I'm going to get people to help me."

He stood up, an ungainly lump of a man. He leaned over the table toward me, still gripping his spoon. "What's evil about the system here, Jack?"

I showed him Ann's scars, explaining what they were and how they had been caused. He laughed.

"You want to come and have a look at my home matrix," he said. "Ever since an unsuccessful revolution ten years ago, the Chinese have employed all scholars in chain gangs. They're busy making roads across the Cairngorms."

"The Chinese? What have they to do with it?"

"The Red Chinese. Didn't they win the Third World War in your matrix?"

"Win it? They didn't even fight it!"

"Well, then, you're just lucky, Jack, and if I were you I'd be inclined to keep my trap shut. Take what's offered, I say!"

Before I had backed out of his room, he was again spooning stew into his mouth.

In the next room was a little plump man, red in the

face and bald of head, who jumped quickly back from fondling his sub girl as I entered with Ann.

"I'm extra-matricial like you," I told him, "and I don't like what I have seen here so far. I hope you feel that these people should not be helped in any way."

"We've rather got to make the best of things now we're here, that's my feeling," he said, coming forward to look at me. "What don't you like about this place?"

"Their system of slavery—of mutilating slaves—it alone is enough to convince anyone that the ruling regime should be overthrown. You must feel the same."

He scratched his bald head, considering the idea.

"You could have worse than slavery, you know. At least slavery guarantees that a part of the population lives above the level of animals. In the Britain of my matrix—and I expect you have found the same—the standard of living has been declining ever since the beginning of the century. So much so that some people are beginning to whisper that communism may not after all be the solution we hoped when it was first generally adopted, and. . . ."

"Communism in Britain? Since when?"

"You sound so surprised, anyone would have thought I said capitalism! After the success of the general strike of 1929, leading to glorious revolution, the first Communist government was established under the leadership of Sir Harold Pollitt. Then in the great People's War of 1940. . . ."

"All right, thanks for the lecture! Just tell me this— will you back me in opposing this regime of slavery?"

"Well, I don't oppose you in opposing it, but first I'd have to confer with the comrades and get a ruling. . . ."

I slammed the door on him. I had backed out hurriedly, and I bumped into another man moving rapidly down the corridor. Brought up short, we regarded each other challengingly. He was young and dark, about my weight and height, with a high bridge to his nose, and I liked the look of him immediately.

"You're an extra-matricial?"

He nodded, smiling gravely, and held out his hand. When I held out mine, he grasped my elbow instead; so I grasped his elbow.

"My name is Mark Claud Gale, at your service. I'm on an errand of revolt, and you look like a possible conscript. None of these spineless fellows will back me up, but I'm not going to give this black-frocked government any help."

"Ah, count me with you all the way, Mark! Great! I am Sherry Meacher, historian and soldier, and I also am recruiting. If we stick together and defy the regime, others may follow our example. And then perhaps the slaves. . . ."

The brazen tongue of a bell interrupted me.

"Time for the historical briefing," Mark said. "Let's go and learn what we can, Sherry, of these altar-kissing hounds! Such knowledge may be turned to our use later. By my shrine, but this is an adventure!"

This aspect of the matter had not struck me before, but to have a sturdy, dependable ally heartened me immensely, and I felt ready for anything. A heady and pleasurable excitement filled me. I could not wait to get to the briefing and to hear, to listen, to be assaulted and insulted by a barrage of new facts that—only a day ago!—would have seemed the wildest fantasy! Then Mark Claud Gale and I would write a page of history of our own.

A pair of dark-clothed church police appeared at the head of the stairs and began ushering us down. The bald man from Communist Britain (but for all I knew there were a million Communist Britains) tagged on with us but did not speak. Ann disappeared as we pressed downstairs. Counting heads, I noted that there were twenty-two of us extra-matricials. As we filed into a hall at the back of the foyer, we found another thirty-odd people awaiting us. From the variety of clothes they were wearing, it was apparent that they were also extra-matricials.

We seated ourselves at long tables on benches and looked to the head table, which stood on a dais and contained three men, each with a secretary, and church police standing behind them. One of the three men was Captain Apostolic Rastell; he gave no sign of having noticed me.

When a bell sounded, one of the men on the dais, a white-haired man of good bearing, rose to his feet and began to speak.

"Gentlemen and sinners, we welcome you to our peaceful Godfearing matrix. We thank you for coming here to bring us help and wisdom. Need I say that your services will be rewarded. I am the Lieutenant Deacon Administered Bligh, and with me are the two members of my committee. Captain Apostolic Rastell is now going to give you a brief history of this matrix so that you may have a correct perspective on our problems. A sub will come round distributing pens and paper to all who wish to make notes."

Rastell rose, bowed slightly to Bligh, and went straight into his talk.

He spoke for almost two hours. From the body of the hall, hardly a whisper came. We listened fascinated to the history of a world like—and yet so hauntingly unlike—ours. Rastell's version was lavishly trimmed by propaganda, yet the man's own personality enlivened even the heaviest passage of dialectic.

A few instances of the strange things Rastell told us must suffice. In this matrix, the concept of nationality has not arisen at as early a date as it had in the matrix I knew. In my home matrix (AA688 Rastell had called it, and I had committed the number to memory), although German and Italian nationality was not achieved until the second half of the nineteenth century, the other great European countries had achieved unity several centuries earlier.

In Rastell's matrix, the kings of England and France had been less successful in their struggles against the feudal lords; one reason for this was, I gathered, that the Church had looked less favorably on the concept of earthly kingdoms. The Church had played the barons against each other and against the Crown. Bishops held more power than kings or parliaments.

Consequently, Great Britain had not become a united kingdom until 1914, at the time of the Franco-German War, in which Britain remained neutral and the Consolidated Holy States of America sold armaments to both sides. In the First World War of 1939, the alignment of power was as I knew it, with a Nazi Germany fighting against Britain and France and, later, Holy Russia and Holy America entering as their allies, while Japan fought on the same side as Germany. Japan, however, had been Christianized. The Americans, having been less attracted to a less heavily industrialized Europe, had turned their attention and their missionaries to Japan earlier than they had done in my matrix.

This led to a crisis in the conduct of the war. American and British scientists developed an atomic bomb. Before using this weapon against their Japanese and German enemies, the thirty-fifth President of the United States, Benedict H. Denning, consulted with the Convocation of Churches.

The Convocation was a powerful group. It not only forbade the use of such a weapon against nominally Christian countries; it gradually took over jurisdiction of the weapon. The war lasted until 1951, by which time the Church was completely in control of all nuclear-power development.

A long and hard war had vitiated the C.H.S.A. and her allies. At the end of the conflict, weak governments fell and a strong church with popular backing rose as a challenging power. Its rule had spread to other countries, particularly to Europe, which was occupied after the war, not by armed forces, but by battalions of militant churchmen.

In 1955, World Church waged a brief nuclear war against China and won.

Since that date, almost a century ago, World Church had kept the fruits and the secrets of nuclear power under her voluminous skirts.

Exhaustion of natural resources had necessitated the employment of subject populations, but there had been no war in the West since 1951. The rule of religion poured out its benefits on to all mankind. What Rastell did not mention were any negative or suppressive results of this rule.

Some of these suppressions were obvious enough. With an autocratic central control and the lack of incentives that wars provide, scientific and technological developments had dropped away. World population, on the other hand, had risen steeply. Rastell mentioned at one point that, after the amalgamation of the Universal Christian Church in 1979, methods of contraception were universally discouraged. The new populations were born into slavery.

"We have been able to turn away from materialism because we have a large subject population to perform the menial tasks of the world for us," Rastell said. It struck me at the time that this was a twisted way of saying that almost every nation without mechanical labor is forced to use slaves.

From what he said, and from what he omitted, it became apparent that almost the only scientific development since the 1960s was the portals, and transmatricial travel. The Church had not encouraged space travel. No doubt they would have been shocked to learn of the Battle of Venus in the Fifth World War, in which I had taken part.

When Rastell had finished speaking, silence lay over the hall. It had grown dusk while he talked; now lights came on reluctantly as we returned to awareness of our own situation. I could see by the faces about me that to many of the extra-matricials, Rastell's material had been more astonishing than I found it.

What amazed me most was the way the Church had departed from what it represented in my matrix. Perhaps it was the possession of nuclear power that had worked the change. Such a possession would have needed strong men to control it, and obviously the strong men had ousted the meek. Another case of absolute power corrupting absolutely. So I said to myself, with the Church cast as villain of the piece. Then Administered Bligh rose again and said nothing to make me doubt my own reasoning.

"Now that you have a perspective with which to work," he said, "World Church can proceed to place before you the problem with which we are immediately faced. As you know, you were brought here to give us your help. All of you are students of history in some form or other, in your separate matrices. A meal is going to be served to you right away; afterward I shall explain our problem in detail and invite your advice; but now I will put it to you in general terms so that you can consider it while you eat.

"We try to instill into our subject population the eternal truth that life in this world is always accompanied by sorrow, alike for those that lead and those that are led, and that they must expect to find their rewards for virtue in the Hereafter. But subs do not learn.

"Several times they have risen against their masters, against World Church. Now—I will tell you frankly, gentlemen—we are faced with a much more serious revolt. The subs have captured the capital; London is in their hands. The Church there was ... somewhat decadent.... The question we are going to ask you, with all its ramifications, is this: will leniency or harshness be the most effective way of dealing with them?

"Should we destroy London with nuclear weapons

and thus risk raising the specter of martyrdom, to inspire other slaves communities? Or should we force them to surrender and forgive them, killing only the ringleaders—thus allowing them to believe that World Church held back not through mercy but weakness?

"Either course is open to us. But we need the benefit of historical knowledge from war-torn matrices to formulate the better solution.

"World Church will bless you for your aid."

He sat down. Already plates were clattering. Subs of both sexes poured forth from doors at the far end of the hall, bearing food. Greasy steam poured from the kitchens, and the smell of porridge and meat.

The little bald man from Communist Britain was sitting next to me.

"An interesting poser, that," he said. "Leniency always impresses the uniformed mind, if it is properly stage-managed."

"Ah, but terror impresses them more," someone else said, and laughed.

"These Church people are dogs, spineless hypocrites," Mark told him. "And you must come from a nasty bootlicking culture if you can seriously give their problem a minute's thought. Don't you agree Sherry?"

He turned his clouded, honest face to me.

"It cheers me immensely to hear that they are having trouble in London, Mark! There are about fifty extra-matricials here. Most of them must feel as we do and will refuse to help this regime. Let's find them and get together...."

Mark held up his hand.

"No, Sherry. Listen, I have a simpler idea!" He leaned forward to speak confidentially. Bald Head also leaned forward to catch his words. Mark put his palm over the man's nose and pushed him away.

"Go away and play in the bushes, smoothpate," he said. To me he said, "Two's never a crowd. An undisciplined bunch of men is nothing but a pain in the kilt. I know, I've had experience. In my own matrix, I'm history instructor in one of our military schools. I've served all over the world—I only got back from legion duty in Kashmir a week before these people grabbed me. Believe me, this paltry Church is used to dealing with slaves, not free men, or they could solve their own problems. The two of us can get away with murder."

"What are you planning?" I had a nasty feeling that I was letting myself in for more trouble than I had bargained for.

"First, we test their resourcefulness. At the same time we get weapons. Can you fight, Sherry? You look like a warrior to me."

"I fought in World War V, on Earth and Venus."

"All these world wars! My matrix is completely different—we only have local campaigns. Much more sensible! Much more civilized! When we have time, we must talk and talk—and listen, of course. First, we must get to the kitchens. Kitchens are always well stocked with weapons, even if these curs are vegetarian. Come on!"

He did not wait for my agreement. He had slipped from the table and was off, bent double so that he could not be seen from the dais. I did the only possible thing. Glad in my heart to be committed, I followed.

Double swing-doors of heavy wood led into the kitchens. We barged in. It was a huge place, bathed in steam, and gave an impression of darkness rather than dirt. All the equipment looked incredibly old-fashioned.

An overseer with a short whip in his hand saw us at once and came toward us. He had a long raw face and sandy eyebrows—yes, an Edinburgh type, I thought—even as I cast about and noted that there was only one other overseer in the whole place, to watch over the activities of perhaps thirty slaves. A plan formed in my mind.

"Leave this fellow to me," I told Mark.

As the overseer came up, with a "What do you gentlemen want, pray?" on his lips, I swung a metal tray from a table at my right hand. The edge of it caught him clean across the bridge of his nose, and he dropped as if dead, without a cry. I saw he had a yellow disc between his shoulder blades.

"I'll get the other foot-kisser," Mark said, clapping my shoulder as he passed.

There were thick-handled mops standing in buckets against one wall. I seized one and ran it through the handles of the doors into the hall. That would hold them temporarily. Another pair of swing doors led to a scullery; I fixed them in the same way. Another door led from the kitchen, a wide door giving on to a courtyard. Pushing a great wooden table, I smashed it against the door and jammed it shut. For a moment, the kitchen was ours!

Turning, I saw that Mark had settled with his overseer. By now the slaves had grasped the fact that something was happening. They stopped their various tasks and stood gaping at us. Grabbing a butcher's knife lying on a bench, I jumped up on to the bench and shouted to them.

"Men, you can all be free! It's a man's right to be free! Better to die than be a slave! Arm yourselves and help us fight those who oppress you. You are not alone. If you help us, others will help you. Now is the time for revenge. Arm yourselves! Fight for your freedom! Fight for your lives!"

I saw Mark turn to me in amazement and horror. Even more surprising was the response of the wretched subs. They knotted together in fear, gazing at me as if I were about to slaughter them. I waved my arms and bellowed at them again. A hammering at the hall doors roused them. Crying, they rushed for it and began to try and tear away my mop, each impeding the other in their anxiety.

Jumping down among them, I pushed them back.

They were flimsy and frightened, falling away from my blows.

"I'm trying to help you! Are you cowards? Don't let them in—they'll kill you. You know they'll kill you. Barricade the doors with the tables! Strike for freedom!"

All they did was shrink back. A few uttered a sort of unvocalized cry. Mark roughly grabbed my arm.

"Sherry, by my shrine, you're crazy! These dogs are born slaves! Dregs! Outcasts! Scum! — Useless to us! They won't fight! — Slaves never do unless they have tasted better days. Leave them, let them be butchered! Arm yourself and let's get out of here."

"But Mark, the whole idea...."

He shoved a great bunched fist under my jaw, swinging it without touching me in time with his words.

"The idea is to overturn this rotting World Church! I know where my duty lies—it lies with the free, not with the servile! Forget this greasy-armed scum! Grab a bigger knife and move. Let's get out of here!"

"But we can't leave these people...."

"You liberal fool, we can and we will! They're dirt, not people!"

He ran across to a long lead sink and pulled a heavy chopping knife from it, tossing it to me. As I caught it, he again bellowed at me to move. His fighting blood was up, his face was scarlet. By now, the hammering on the kitchen door had grown in volume. They would be breaking in at any moment. The slaves cowered in a group nearby, watching Mark and me anxiously. Some crossed themselves. I turned and ran after Mark.

He pointed to a large service elevator in one corner. We rushed to it.

"It only leads upstairs!"

"That'll do. Get in and haul on the rope!"

We jumped into the cumbersome contraption. It

could be maneuvered from inside by the ropes that supported it.

"Hey, stop! Wait for me!"

At the shout, both Mark and I turned. The overseer I had laid out with the tray was staggering toward us.

"Let me join you," he said. "I'd sooner die than carry on as I am. I'll fight on your side. I'm for you!"

"You're an overseer. We don't want you!" I said.

"No, wait," Mark said. "He is a promoted slave, isn't that right, fellow? They have plenty of fight in them because they've learned the difference between better and worse. Climb in, man, and be welcome. You can show us the layout of this infernal place."

The overseer jumped in beside us and helped us haul on the ropes. We creaked up into darkness. As we bent to the task, Mark said, "We want church police uniforms as quickly as possible. Then we can walk out of the building unnoticed!"

"Och, that should be easy enough," grunted the overseer. "Friends, whether we meet with death or daylight, my name's Andy Campbell, and I'm glad to be in your company."

"We're Mark and Sherry, and that tray was not delivered in anger."

"Man, I'd thought you'd cut my skull into two pieces! I must work off my sorrow on a churchgoer as soon as possible."

He hadn't long to wait before he did that.

We emerged on a poorly lighted landing; a portly man in gaiters and some sort of ecclesiastical garb was passing the hatchway. As he turned, saw us, and opened his mouth to shout, I was on him. He gave a shout before I could bring him to the ground, and a police officer appeared almost immediately. I'll never forget his look of horrified surprise as he rounded the corner and came upon three wild men. He went for his gun far too late. Andy was there, sinking a steel blade through his jacket, through his chest, into his heart. He died with a look of surprise still frozen on his face.

"Ah, blood of the bull, neatly done, my noble lads!" Mark exclaimed, smacking his fist into his palm. He pulled open a nearby door, and we dragged the two bodies into the room. A wood fire burned in an old-fashioned grate. It looked as if the occupant of the room might be back shortly.

"We've got two good sets of clothing here," I said. "You two climb into them if they'll fit. I'll see what's going on outside. I'm sure you wouldn't want anyone to catch you with your trousers down."

The portly man in gaiters was unconscious. Andy gagged him before beginning to strip off his clothes.

Prowling in the corridor, I could hear a din from below, rising up the elevator shaft. We were in the thick of trouble, and the knowledge delighted and excited me. When I got to the head of the stairs, I heard footsteps and knew someone was almost at the top of them, ascending rapidly but quietly. A sort of broom closet on wheels stood near me; hurriedly I slid behind it, into the shadows.

Whoever it was had gained the landing. A sort of fury to attack—based perhaps on fear—overcame me. I heaved the closet away from the wall and flung myself out. Falling, the closet struck the newcomer, sending him spinning against the wall. I was at his throat and had my thumbs deep in his windpipe before I realized it was Rastell.

"Mark!" I called. Mark appeared almost at once, and we dragged Rastell into our room and shut the door. Mark drew his knife.

"Don't kill him, Mark. I know him."

"Know him? He's our enemy, Sherry. Let me skewer him and you can wear his uniform. It looks about your size."

"Aye, skewer him, or I will," Andy said. "Death to the Church!"

"Leave him alone," I said. "His name's Rastell. He's

okay. We'll strip him and leave him tied up here, but I won't see him killed."

"Well, hurry up," said Mark, and he and Andy lowered their knives. They were disguised now, their own clothes tossed on to the floor.

Rastell's face had turned ashy. He made no protest as I dragged off his jacket and trousers. I hated to see him look so craven.

"Remember what you said, Rastell? 'Men spend large parts of their lives awaiting a challenge.' Well, here it is!"

He did not answer a word. As I tugged his garments on I turned to Mark.

"What's the plan? They'll be searching this floor any moment."

"These Church people aren't efficient or they'd never have failed to post guards over us in the hall. They had no particular reason to think we should be friendly. But they can get mobilized against us more quickly than we can gather a force together against them. So we must leave Edinburgh."

"Hey, devil's luck, there's a police car outside! We could steal that and join the rebellion in London, if either of you can drive," Andy Campbell said. He was over by the window, peering out at the back of the building.

"In my matrix, transport is publicly owned, and I'm no driver," I said.

"In mine, one learns to drive as part of the initiation rites at puberty," Mark said. Going to stare down at the car with Andy, he said, "We'll try it! Hurry up and get those clothes on, Sherry. But we won't try for London. We must leave Edinburgh the way we came—by the portal machines. The one that brought me here was up on Arthur's Seat, and there were others beside it. We'll drive there at once. Once we get back to our own worlds—Andy, you come to mine with me—we muster aid there, then reappear in London and join the rebellion, armed and properly prepared to fight. My government would welcome the chance!"

I was sure my government would not, vitiated as the nation's resources were after a long war, but in outline Mark's plan was a good one. It was no time to argue over details. Having buttoned up Rastell's tunic over my chest, I ripped a length of cord from the blind on the window and tied Rastell to the bars at the back of the cumbersome sofa. As I finished doing this, something creaked in the corridor. We all three turned to the door at once.

"It's the elevator going down!" Andy exclaimed. "Come on, Sherry, they're on to us!"

With a whoop, Mark grabbed a heavy rug that lay before the fire. Burying his hands in it, he seized the fire basket out of the fireplace and ran with it blazing and smoking out of the room. He flung it; and burning logs, basket, and rug went flying down the shaft after the elevator. Hardly pausing, he ran to the top of the stairs with us after him. We raced down together.

A half-dozen church police, revolvers at the ready, came charging along the lower corridor. We met them at the bottom of the stairs. Before Mark could do anything rash, I gripped his arm and called to the police, pointing wildly back up the stairs as I did so, "Quickly, they're up there—second floor! Six of them! Cover them while we go and get the hoses!"

The police burst past us, galloping up the stairs. The look of delight on Andy's face! As we ran to the rear exit, we could hear screams from the direction of the kitchen. I wondered if the elevator was on fire or if the slaves were being lashed for letting us through.

We broke out into a courtyard, under surveillance from a hundred windows. Although it was dark, several subs were about, unloading meat from a van, lighting their way with long, waxy torches. Nearer to us stood the car we had seen from the upper window; a policeman in the black and white uniform sat at the wheel holding a paper, but looking uneasily about. As

I wrenched open his door, he flung the paper in my face and fumbled for his gun. Yelling like a savage, I threw all my weight on him, knocking him sideways across the seat, springing on top of him. Andy had piled into the back seat. His hands came over to grasp the wretched man around the neck. At the same moment, the gun exploded.

Its noise, breaking only a foot away from my ear, seemed almost enough to kill me by itself, though the bullet tore through the roof. The man was struggling violently under me, but for the present I could do nothing; all fight had gone out of me. I lay across the policeman while Andy choked the life out of him.

While they were struggling, Mark started the car. His hands ran all over the controls as he tested their functions. The vehicle bucked violently. He cursed it, then it moved forward. In a daze, I saw what happened next.

Two police officers came dashing out of a doorway slightly ahead of us. The gunshot had brought them. They were armed only with short swords. Without a pause, they both jumped onto the running board on the near side of the car. Some of the narrow windows were open, and so they clung there.

One managed to draw his sword, thrusting it inside at Andy, who still struggled with my man. Andy let go and grasped the wrist that held the sword.

As if in slow motion, as we rolled forward, I saw the other hanger-on unsheath his sword and bring it through the window, preparing to finish Andy before he finished me. I could do nothing. The concussion of the explosion so near my head still left me dazed. I just slumped there, staring at that well-tended sword blade as it stabbed toward Andy.

Gathering speed, Mark twisted the wheel. We headed for the meat vans. Slaves shrieked and scattered. Mark swerved again, missing the other vehicle by inches. Agony distorted the faces of our two hangers-on. Their heads twisted, their mouths gaped open, their swords dropped, as they were crushed between the two vehicles and fell away from our sight.

Andy was patting us both on the back and cheering. He produced a small flask of whiskey—which he found in the hip pocket of the ecclesiastical trousers he had commandeered—and made me take a sizable swig. My throat burned and I felt better.

The fellow I was half-lying on was unconscious. Together, Andy and I dragged him over into the back seat.

"This is a crazy car to drive," Mark said, but he was doing well. We were clear on to the streets now. There was no sign of alarm. Mark was driving slowly so as not to excite attention.

The streets were poorly lighted, and there was little traffic. I had no idea of the time; it could not have been later than eight o'clock, yet hardly a soul was to be seen. The slaves, I thought, probably had a curfew; they were probably in bed or at prayers.

"It'll be wonderful to get another place to live," Andy said. "and while I think of it, slow down, Mark, and turn right, here, up Hanover Street. There's a big government store at the top.—Peace Militant it's called—that supplies only to officials, I've heard. One of the fellows in the kitchen had to work there once. If we can get in there, for sure it'll be shut, and we can get in and find some of these portals and slip out of this matrix at once."

"Mark had the idea we should get to Arthur's Seat."

Andy swore "That lousy dump! It'll be swarming with Church Army The Peace store will be safer."

That settled it.

Mark shifted gear, and we growled uphill. Off Princes Street lights were few and far between. At the top of the road we found the store It was a great solid granite block with little pinchpenny ecclesiastical windows in which goods darkly lay. A board above a barred door said Peace Militant.

And Andy groaned.

At that moment I was taking another mouthful of whiskey. I turned to see what was the matter. The man he had half-strangled had revived and thrust a knife between his ribs. He was withdrawing the blade as I turned. Dim lights shone on the blade, and by that same tawdry glow I saw his teeth as he growled and came at me. I was already at him with the bottle.

The heel of it caught him in the eye. Involuntarily, he brought his hand up, and I grasped his wrist and wrenched the knife from his grip. He yelped. My fury was back. Tumbling over the seat at him, I bore him down into the darkness, while the knife—his own knife—sunk down and carried him into a night from which there would never be a dawn.

I found Mark was shaking me. The car had stopped.

"You did a good job, boy, but he can die only once, worse luck! Leave him! Come on, we've got to get into the shop quickly before they catch up with us."

"He's killed Andy. Andy Campbell's dead!"

"I'm sorry about it too. Weeping won't help it. Andy's dog's meat now. Come on, Sherry, you're a real warrior. Let's move!"

I got out onto the pavement. Mark stove in a window with his elbow, and we climbed through. As simple as that! The terrible feeling of excitement was on me, a state of possession.

We began tramping through the store.

The ground floor yielded nothing, though we separated and searched. We were about to go upstairs, when I found a floor directory. In the light filtering in from outside, I read a line that ran: Basement: Tropical Plants, Gardens, Café, Library, Extra-Matricial Equipment. Mark and I took the stairs at a run.

Below ground, we thought it safe enough to switch on a couple of lights. Here was the first evidence I had seen that this civilization boasted some sort of

aesthetic sense. Heating was on, and in the warmth
basked a perfect tropical garden. Flowering trees and
shrubs, a line of banana plants, gaudy hibiscus, rioted
here in carefully tended disorder. The centerpiece
was a pool on which lilies floated and the lights were
reflected back in dark water.

Beyond the pool, the café had been arranged with
tables and chairs set on a terrace overlooking the
pool. Attractive, I thought, and we pushed past the
chairs and came to the adjoining department. Here
stood a dozen portals made in several different sizes
and models.

We both cheered up, dropped our knives, and got
to work.

This was something about which we knew nothing.
We had much to learn before we could return to our
own worlds. To my relief, the portals we came across
first were primed for immediate sale and contained
vials of nicomiotine, as well as other drugs. There
were instruction manuals provided, and we sat down
to master their contents with what patience we had.

The business of returning to one's own matrix
turned out to be fairly simple. One had a preliminary
injection of a fluid with a complicated name which
seemed to be a kind of tranquilizer, followed by a jab
of nicomiotine in the stated quantity according to
one's size/age ratio, and then sat in the portal seat,
the vibratory rate of which could be adjusted to matrix numbers shown on a dial. When the drugs took
and the body's vibratory rate reached the correct
pitch, the return was effected.

"These people may have established a loathsome
social order, but this invention is something to their
credit," I said. "And if they would only educate and
liberate their slaves, I can't help admiring any matrix
that has escaped with not more than one world war."

"We've had no world wars," Mark growled.

"Then you look at it differently, but for the
slaves. . . ."

"Sherry, you keep talking about slaves. I'm tired of the subject. By the Phrygian birth, forget all about them! In every matrix there must be conquerers and conquered, dogs and masters. It's a law of human nature."

I dropped the instruction manual and stared.

"What are you saying? We have only done what we have done, fought as we have, for the sake of the poor wretches enslaved here. What else did we fight for?"

He was crouching beside me. His face set hard. His words fell from his lips like little graven images.

"I have done nothing for any slaves. What I have done has been against the Church."

"As far as that goes, I'm pretty startled by its conduct too. In my matrix, the Christian Church is a power for good. Although it condones war, its tenets. . . ."

"Death to the Christian Church! It's the Christian Church I fight against!" He jumped to his feet. I leaped up too, my own anger awakened by his words, and we stood glaring at each other.

"You're crazy, Mark! We may not agree with the Church, but it has been the established church in Britain now for centuries. To start. . . ."

"Not in my Britain! It's not established in my Britain! Christianity is the faith of dogs and underlings where I come from. When Rastell started to tell us his history, he talked about the Roman Empire being established in the East by Constantine the Great, and he said that Constantine, followed by an emperor he called Theodosius, installed Christianity as the official creed of the Empire. Did it happen that way in your matrix?"

"Yes, just as Rastell said."

"Well, it didn't happen that way in mine! I know of this man you call Constantine; we call him Flavius Constantinus. Of Theodosius I have not heard. Constantinus was killed by his father-in-law Maximian and never became emperor. Maxentius the Great became emperor after Diocletian."

I was puzzled now, as well as angry. Gibbon no doubt would have been delighted to hear of this setback for Christianity, but its implications left me baffled.

"All this was seventeen centuries ago. What has it to do with us?"

He was rigid with hostility.

"Everything, my friend—everything! In your matrix and in this one, Christianity was imposed on the West by your two misguided emperors. In mine, Christianity was stamped out, though it still survives among the barbarians and slaves whom we rule in the East, and the True Religion was fostered and grew, and flourishes irresistibly!"

"The True Religion?"

"By my shrine, Sherry, have you never heard of the soldier's god? Then bow down before the name of Mithras!"

I saw it then, saw above all my criminal stupidity in thinking that because we seemed to have a common purpose we might have a common past. This man, with whom I had spent the fiercest hour of my life, was my enemy!

How much of an enemy I saw before he did, and there lay my only advantage. He was less clear about conditions in my matrix than I was now about his. I saw that he would go back to his matrix and probably return with legions of warriors to tumble the unwarlike Church regime here. Though I wanted slavery abolished, I did not want that.

The thought of intermatricial war and conquest was horrifying. Knowledge of the portals must never get back to his Mithraic world. The conclusion was obvious—I had to kill Mark Claud Gale!

He saw murder in my eyes before I reached him. He was quick, Mark! As he stooped to grasp his knife, I kicked it flying and caught his shoulder with my knee. He fell, taking me with him, his fingers digging into my calf. A personal wrestle was what I did not want; he was probably in better condition than I. A weapon was what I wanted!

As his right hand came up to grasp me, I planted my free knee in his windpipe and wrenched his arm down hard over it, at the same time pulling myself loose from his grasp. Jumping up, I ran into the artificial garden.

Behind the café were rows of garden tools on display. He hurled a can at me before I reached them. The can struck my shoulder and bounced through the front of the café in a shower of glass.

I turned. He was almost on me! I kicked one of the light tables between us and backed off to the tool racks. Feeling the shaft of one of the tools behind me, I brought it forward, flinging my weight with it as if it were a lance. I had hold of a rake. It struck Mark in the thigh as he jumped aside.

I had time to make another lunge, but he had the other end of the rake. Next moment, we were struggling face to face. He brought his skull down hard on my nose. Pain and fury burst like a volcanic eruption over me. I caught him by the throat, jabbing him in the groin with my knee. He hooked a leg around my other leg and jerked it. As I fell, I stamped on his instep. He doubled in pain, leaving the back of his neck unprotected. Even as I chopped the side of my hand down on it, I felt the weakness of my blow. I was dizzy from the pain in my face.

We broke apart. The rake lay between us. Gathering my strength, I turned, snatched another tool from the rack behind, and swung it in a circle. He had stooped to grab the rake. Changing his mind, he backed away, and I ran at him with the tool upraised. It was a fool's move. I broke the shaft over his shoulders as we fell backward into the ornamental pool.

The water was warm, but the shock of it helped me

to keep my senses. The pool was about three feet deep. I floundered to my feet, beating off slimy lily stalks, still grasping one end of the tool. I was bellowing for breath like a hungry sea lion.

Mark took longer to surface. From the way he moved, from the way his left arm hung limp and he clutched his shoulder, I knew I had broken something useful. He turned away from me and headed for the opposite bank, where banana trees and tall grasses grew.

Compassion rose in me. I had no heart to go on. Had he not been my ally? But in that moment of weakness, he turned and looked at me. I understood that look. We were enemies, and he was going for a weapon with which to kill me. There would be plenty about: pruning knives, shears, blades of all kinds. I could not let him get away.

He dragged himself onto the bank, using only one arm.

The broken half of the garden tool in my hand was the business end of some sort of edging implement, with a sharp crescent-shaped blade. I threw it hard.

Mark swayed and grasped at the banana tree. He missed. He tried to reach the shaft in his back with his good hand, but failed. He fell back into the pool and disappeared among the reeds. There was a good deal of thrashing about in the water, but it stopped at last. I climbed out of the pool.

Staggering, gasping incoherently, I made for the portals.

It is useless to ask me how I went through the vanishing routine. I don't know. Somehow I did all that was necessary, injected myself, tuned my portal. As I sat in the seat, I could hear noises outside the store, distant and meaningless, and the sound of a door being broken down, and the squeal of whistles. Then the effect overcame me.

Blackness. Blankness.

And—I was sprawling on a crowded night-club

floor with three half-naked dancers shrieking their heads off in fright! I was back home!

They threw me out of the club without bothering to ask questions. Just as well! One thing I could not have told them: I could not remember the classification number of the matrix from which I had escaped. There was no going back there, except by accident. Rastell's world was lost among a myriad of others in the multidimensional universe.

This fortunate bit of ignorance saved me from a severe moral problem. Supposing we could have gotten back to Rastell's world, had we in fact any right to intervene on behalf of the slaves? Should we cultivate someone else's garden? In any one world, there's enough trouble in circulation without looking for it in others. Or so I explained the situation to Candida.

She pulled her moral face at me. Recovering from the influenza she had contracted at Noordoostburg-op-Langedijk, her pallor made her moral face even more moral than usual.

"I am well enough to attend evensong in St. Giles today, Sheridan," she said. "And I suggest you come with me. After your unholy adventures in that benighted matrix, you are plainly in need of absolution in this one."

At that time, I believed that she meant merely that the killing of Mark in self-defense lay upon my conscience; and since it did, I meekly bowed to her suggestion.

I spent the day resting up. In the evening, as dusk settled over our festering old city, and before Royal and Turton could return home from work, Candida and I slipped down into the crowded streets and made our way up the hill to the grand old Gothic pile of Edinburgh's cathedral.

Resourceful little Candida led me by a shortcut down a slype between blank damp-stained walls. It was so narrow, we could not walk side by side; I went after her, noticing anew how slight was this strong-willed little fey sister-in-law. Footsteps sounded behind us—someone was catching up to us—a hand grasped my shoulder. I spun about, instinctively raising my fists, and stared into a strong square face with intense dark eyes. When I had last seen that face, it had quailed before death in fear, but there was no fear in it now.

"Captain Apostolic Rastell!"

"I am Captain Apostolic no longer," he said. "I am a man on the run—as you are!" He gave me a hard scrutinizing look as I pressed back against the wall.

Candida had stopped and was examining him haughtily.

"So this is one of your friends from that disgraceful matrix, Sherry. . . . Well, aren't you going to introduce me to him?"

With Candida, one always remembered one's manners. Only when I had performed hurried introductions did I ask Rastell, "What do you mean by saying I am on the run? I am safe and in my proper matrix! I never thought to see you again! You are the fugitive here!"

"You are a fugitive as much as I!" He clutched my arm. "Is there somewhere that we can talk?"

"There is nowhere," Candida declared. "We are on our way to divine service. You may join us if you care to—and from what I hear of the goings-on in your dimension, you *should* care to, for the sake of your soul. After service, you can talk to Sheridan."

"As safe there as anywhere, I suppose," Rastell said, half to himself.

After the service, it was Candida who pointed out that the cathedral itself was the best place in which to talk. Perhaps she had no wish for Royal's interference at that stage. But Rastell was convinced by the swarms of anonymous worshipers, and by the great darkness that towered up through the somber and fretted interior—a darkness which the meager lighting could do no more than punctuate.

Persuaded by this general obscurity, if not by my sister-in-law, Rastell led us from the side chapel into the Moray aisle. Lurking under Moray's monument, he said, addressing us both, "Insurrection is now rife in my home matrix! No, not the subs, poor craven things—it's the extra-matricials we brought in who are causing the trouble. And you began that trouble, Sheridan Meacher!"

"I'm delighted to hear that things are going so well!"

"Things are going badly with you, never think otherwise! Both church police and Matrix Corps are already on your track, combing the nearest matrices. They are determined that you shall die for your part in the insurrection."

"Why do you come to warn me, Rastell? We are no friends!"

"Church knows, that is the truth. Yet you spared my life, Meacher. And I too am on the run. I was lucky to escape. They will have my blood for what they call my inefficiency—so I also have to get away from them."

I looked up bewildered, my eye catching the horrible stained-glass window representing Moray being murdered and John Knox grimly reading his funeral oration, to which the fading daylight lent stark emphasis. To be food for a similar oration was as yet far from my desire.

"Why have you bothered to come and inform Sherry of all this, Mr. Rastell?" Candida asked.

He turned to her. "Because he is the only person I know outside my own matrix—because we must cooperate if we are to escape death."

"And how do you propose to do that?"

"Why, we must flee together to another matrix, one far from our own probability line, and lie low there for a few months—longer if necessary—until they grow tired of searching for us."

"I see," said Candida, in a tone that could have

frozen John Knox. "From that, I deduce that you have near at hand one of these extra-matricial portals and that you intend to whisk my brother-in-law away through it."

"Correct, madam."

"You will do no such thing! We are a small but devoted family. I will not have Sherry disappear into matrices even more perverted than ours. He has got himself into enough unholy trouble already."

"He is in danger here."

"He would be in danger there." They stared at each other in the waning light. I did not know what to say. Finally, Candida said, "There is a solution. I shall come with you. Through the portal."

"Madam!"

"Both of you are weak in the faith. I shall accompany you and see that you do not fall into sin. Lead on, Mr. Rastell!"

Rastell had left his portal in a seamy room in a lodginghouse not far from the church. He assembled it as Candida and I stood by. I tried to argue her out of her decision as Rastell prepared the nicomiotine injections, but she was adamant.

"You have already made clear your somewhat lax attitude to other matrices, Sherry. 'There's enough trouble in circulation in our world without going looking for it in others.' That's what you said. I disagree. Christ's teaching shows that we are morally responsible for everyone. If they are human and have souls to lose, then the people in other matrices are as we are, whether they happen to live in another dimension or not."

"But they have their own standards! Our moral obligation is to not judge them by our moral standards."

"*Our* moral standards? They are not ours, but come from On High. We merely follow them; and we must see that others follow them. The standards exist in their own right, whether acknowledged or not, just as God does."

The Meacher family enjoys such arguments and takes them up at a moment's notice, like embroidery.

Rastell had brought out a small black notebook and was looking up classification numbers.

"Then we will escape to a matrix far from this, where no God has ever been acknowledged on Earth," he said. There must have been irony in his voice, but Candida said eagerly, "There is such a matrix? Then indeed we can be of some positive good there!" She clapped her hands.

Rastell put her through the portal first. I went next. He came last, and I saw he materialized carrying the portal, like a circus clown who jumps through his own hoop. But I had no time to ponder this minor wonder of science, for Candida was already involved in a flaming row with an inhabitant of our new matrix!

The matrix or the inhabitant? Which to start with? The inhabitant—I had better not refer to him as a Scot—claimed all of Candida's attention, and so it was on him I looked first, and he shall be first described.

He was an undersized specimen, of brutal demeanor, with coarse hair that I suspected covered all his barrel-body under its coarse clothing. Evidently, he had grasped Candida as soon as she materialized. He was chattering at her in a language I could not understand—and getting the worst of the battle, for she was clouting him with the heavy shopping bag she had carried to church. Even as I ran to tackle her assailant, he broke away.

Just for a moment, he bent and made a gesture of such animal obscenity that Candida shrieked in indignation. Then he made off downhill fast, running flat-footedly along the paved street.

I say street—track would be a better word. For this Edinburgh—our fair Auld Reekie—hardly resembled in any way except the characteristic lie of the land the city of my or Rastell's dimension. The houses appeared to be merely senseless accumulations of stones and branches of trees. The street, as I say, was a mere track between these shacks and was piled with refuse and human droppings. Where, in our matrix, St. Giles had stood, was a rough building, almost like a crude parody of a church, with a sort of spire that on closer inspection proved to be the apex of a dead fir tree.

All this I could see because here it was happily still only midafternoon, and I resolved that we should be gone by dusk. Whatever had befallen the miserable inhabitants of Earth here, I saw no reason why we should inflict their lot on ourselves.

"So this is what a world is like without belief in the Lord!" exclaimed Candida. "The heathens! They look and act like godless ones! Yes, the devil rules here. Be off!"

This last was directed at a group of capering loons who had collected to see the fun. They jumped up and down with glee, cackled, turned cartwheels, mimicked our actions.

I turned to Rastell. "They're a pack of apes! Nothing but a pack of apes! What sort of trick is this? You've shot us into a kind of prehistoric matrix, haven't you?"

"No, it is no trick. This is a matrix exactly contemporary with ours. Only the human race has taken a different path."

"Away from God!" said Candida. "If only I could speak their language!"

A piece of filth hit her on the shoulder. Our spectators—perhaps angered by the dullness of our performance—had started to throw things. I grasped Candida around the shoulders and urged her away. The spectators bunched fingers at both ends of their long lipless mouths and whistled in derision— wonderful, long, whooping, spiky, swooping, whistles;

wish I could do it! With Rastell following, we hurried between two of the fetid shacks, nearly tripping over droves of little hairy black pigs as we went.

And there Edinburgh ended, in mud and wretched fields. What I knew as Cowgate was unkempt agricultural land. And it was being worked! Two groups were at work, engaged in some sort of plowing operation. Above the plow itself sat, in each case, an ape overseer on a perch, which he grasped with his feet while wielding a crude thong whip over the backs bent before him. In one group, these backs were many: puny little monkey backs, where a dozen simian captives sought to drag the plow through the stony ground. In the other group, the back was but one: a broad black back, as some immense creature like an overgrown gorilla tugged at the shafts that moved the furrowing blade.

The magnificent horror of the scene got through to me at once. Only later did I see its significance and guess that this was a form of agriculture involving the use of captives of other tribes. The little figures toiled below tatty gray and fawn clouds bringing rain.

We had not long to look, for a straggle of weird shapes was progressing from behind the shacks toward us. Rastell held out a warning hand.

"No point in running. They will not hurt us."

"Who was going to run?" Candida asked indignantly. "We must learn their language and set to work converting them to Christianity. Nothing else can lift them from this animal state."

"I don't believe they have language as we know it," Rastell said.

The people approaching were long-legged and grotesque. Everything was so strange there that only when they had surrounded us did I realize that they went on stilts. There were six of them. All wore a kind of uniform. Since I was frantically trying to relate everything in that matrix to something in ours,

I mistook the uniform for black leather, such as the young toughs of my Edinburgh wear; later I came to the firm conclusion that it must be the skin of their adversaries, the gorilla-people.

The people—no, let's say the ape-people, for so they were—the ape-people were using stilts about three feet high, which they manipulated very cleverly with their feet, leaving their hands free. When one reached out for my shoulder, I put up my hand sharply, and he at once was down to the ground and, swinging his stilt as a weapon without changing "hands," dealt me a considerable blow in the ribs—and in a twinkling had resumed his stilt walk.

"They won't attack you if you don't scare them!" Rastell said.

"How can you be sure?" Candida asked.

"Because they are not hostile like human beings, only suspicious like apes."

"Well, I'm both!"

But we allowed ourselves to be herded along docilely enough, for the stilt-walkers achieved what was evidently their aim, cowing us by overtopping us. The august effect was spoiled only by their chatter—at which I saw Candida frowning concentratedly, as if trying to distinguish words.

The stilt-walkers herded us up to the large shack that stood like a mockery where our fine Gothic cathedral was in the home matrix. Four of them took up positions by the entrance. The other two pushed us in, jumping deftly down from their stilts as they got inside.

Although dim, the interior was fairly large, as it had need to be, for a whole family of ape-people was here. With a dim memory of monkey behavior, I thought I could distinguish several old males squatting in the background, as well as more active females, who moved about in coarse frocks of garish yellow which did not cover their posteriors. There were also children swarming here, though taking care to keep away from—I marveled that they had such an amenity!—a small fire burning to one side in a hollowed rock. The smells that assailed us were rich and strange.

Almost above our heads hung a trapeze. Sitting negligently on it, chewing a carrot, was a hefty young male. His black uniform was decorated with bright feathers, while around his ankles, I saw, he had two dangerous-looking spurs tied. He was glaring at us.

The stilt-walkers beside us had fallen to the floor and were groveling and uttering low moans.

"This is the boss," I said.

"We'd better kneel, just to show we're friendly," Rastell said. "Once we're accepted—no trouble."

"Quite right! If we are to teach him humility, we must be prepared to humble ourselves," Candida said. She looked at me severely. "Kneel, Sherry!" Thus, I believe, the kindly woman saved my face; I could obey her.

But as we were all going down, the boss above spat a piece of carrot which caught Rastell in the eye. He was up in an instant, forgetting discretion.

"You baboon!" he called, shaking his fist.

It was immediately grasped. Before I could even leap up, the brute on the trapeze had swung Rastell right up, effortlessly, until for a moment their two faces were almost touching. There was a flash of canine teeth, we heard a cry, Rastell was tumbling unsupported to the ground. He sprawled. I saw his ear was bleeding. It had been torn by the boss's teeth.

The boss himself, snarling and spitting, landed lightly a few paces away, and was now advancing on Rastell, swinging his arms, leaping up and down, chattering. The children had all scattered back to their mothers, who huddled nervously together, saying nothing.

There was going to be a fight.

Jumping up, I grabbed at one of the stilts lying by a prostrate guard. They were at once upon me. I swung the stick hard, striking them madly, but the gorilla hide protected them and they bore me down. I was flattened ignominiously, and the stilt twisted from my grip. They held me down, face pressed into the filthy ground, waiting like trained dogs for word from the master.

Their master was still circling Rastell. Rastell had picked himself up and was looking hopelessly around for a weapon. His ear was scattering blood. I saw that two old males had lumbered up from the back and held Candida, clumsily but not viciously. The females in the corner were whooping and leaping.

Then there was silence and the tableau held. The boss was about to spring, to throw himself, teeth and spurs, on Rastell, when the latter moved.

He bent down, almost into a crouch, touching the ground with his elbows, and smacked his lips. His body was presented sideways to the boss. The stance made him resemble an ape. The boss advanced and hesitated—we were all tense—and then jumped to the rear of Rastell. Momentarily, he seized him around the ribs and clouted him, and then he broke free. Rastell stood up.

All tension had disappeared. Candida and I were allowed to stand free. We brushed ourselves down; Rastell mopped his face and his ear. The children and the female ape-people began running and chattering again. As for the boss, he had lost interest in us. Whooping to the guards, he sprang onto his trapeze again. In a moment, we three human beings were led into the open again.

The stilt-walkers hustled us along to the end of the street and there, with gestures and calls, plainly said good-bye.

I shook Rastell's hand. "You were quick-witted in

there. You adopted ape-behavior and so probably saved us all from being killed."

"It was disgusting to see you kowtow to an animal," Candida said.

Laughing, Rastell said, "Aren't they our superiors in many ways? They have no interspecies fighting or killing, as men have. I merely observed their tribal customs."

"Our superiors, Mr. Rastell? Those godless beasts? No wonder they have not advanced from the ape if they have never found religion!"

"We can discuss that point at our leisure later, Mrs. Meacher," Rastell said coldly. Turning to me, he added, "Now we've got a short walk."

A little herd of idlers had gathered and was running about us, whistling, calling, and mocking. They all dropped away as we set off from the village. I put my arm around Candida's shoulder to encourage her. The afternoon was growing very drab; rain threatened; and we were far from home. It was clear that we had passed some sort of inspection in the crude village and were now allowed to go free in this primitive world; clear, too, that Rastell knew what he was about; yet both Candida and I were reluctant to ask him questions.

As we walked westward, following a track leading beneath the rocky outcrop on which—in any sane matrix—sat Edinburgh Castle, I was thinking hard. Rastell was not to be trusted. The episode with that Mithras-lover, Mark Claud Gale, had warned me against alliances where unknown factors were involved.

Rastell's objectives were not mine, however he tried to make it look that way; and I clearly understood that the time when our objectives were to be revealed as opposed was approaching. Rastell was taking us for no afternoon stroll. We were purposefully going somewhere. And I could guess, at least in outline, the sort of place it would be.

I had no weapon. Rastell had a sidearm. He had not used it on the leader of the ape-people. So there was an arrangement of some sort with the ape-people. Rastell was familiar with this matrix.

No. I was guessing. No proof; it could merely be my fears prompting me. And if my fears were unfounded, then I needed to cooperate with this man. He could be the only man in the whole matrix ... but I doubted that.

As we walked, I watched him.

He was marching stolidly ahead, leading us toward the Water of Leith, which probably existed in this matrix as it did in his and mine. Candida, still obsessed with religious aspects, was talking volubly to him; Rastell hardly seemed to be listening.

"... all more terrible than anything I could imagine! You seem to understand their way of behaving—if we are to be here long, I also must try to understand them, to speak their language, so that I can bring the word of God to them. You will help, won't you, Mr. Rastell, as a man of God yourself?"

"They're better left as they are."

"How can you say that? How dare you say it? Isn't this entire matrix a proof of the power of God's love? They don't have it here—and they've stayed on the level of animals for a million years! We must bring Christ to them."

Rastell turned to her blank-faced and solid; no gleam there. "Think again, Mrs. Meacher! These people haven't developed as we have. We progressed from their man-ape stage, didn't we? We—our ancestors—became hunters after the arboreal phase, and from hunters on to higher organizations. Where do you think God entered the arrangement, Mrs. Meacher?"

"God created the world."

He laughed, bitter and dragging, as if the sound hurt him.

"No, the reverse is true! Our world created God. In

the arboreal stage, the monkey stage, where this matrix has stuck, there's no need for God."

"No need! You don't mean. . . ."

"Monkeys have no need for God, I tell you. Instead, each group has a boss, a leader, a tyrant, like the one we just met. He makes the law, dispenses rough justice, performs all the societal roles of your God. But when apes branch out into hunters and compete for food with clever carnivores like wolves, they have to reject such tyranny, because each member of the pack has to think for himself. So the leader's authority has to loosen. So he invents a shadow behind him, a supreme authority, in which all can believe. A moral law is intruded to keep order where before a fist ruled. A god is invented."

"Idols! Graven images!"

"At first, yes. Then more sophisticated gods, gods omnipotent and invisible and angry—And finally—God! Jehovah!"

We had scrambled down the banks of a little gorge. Before us flowed the narrow river called the Water of Leith. But in my time, it had been spanned by Telford's beautiful bridge. Now there was nothing there but a rotten little ferry—a flat-bottomed boat that could be dragged from one bank to the other by means of a wire secured across the stream. And I saw at once that even that humble arrangement was the work of men, not ape-people.

On the far bank, confirming all I suspected, stood a barbed-wire fence; there was a locked gate in it, directly opposite the ferry.

The rain began to fall. It was a moment of purest chill.

Candida was saying, numbly, to Rastell, "You claim God is merely man's invention to back his own authority! You, a Godfearing man!"

"Keep quiet—we're almost there. Get into the boat. And you. . . ."

Before he could finish, I dived sideways and grabbed at his gun. He struck my arm. I grasped him around the waist; he fought savagely and we sprawled to the ground.

I was on top of him, a knee in his stomach. With both hands, I grasped him around the throat, just as I had once before. His torn ear began to seep blood again. His thumbs came up, gouging at my eyes; his face was livid under my pressure. Candida pulled his gun free and rammed its muzzle against his ear.

"Lie still or I'll kill you!"

I knew she would. So did he! He lay flat, the fight knocked out of him.

Roughly, I rolled him over and started to untie the portal from his back.

"Sheridan," he said hoarsely, "I'm taking you to safety, I swear!"

"You swear, what do you swear by? By your honor? By God? You believe in nothing but power, Rastell—you've explained your philosophy to us. Anything is justified if it reinforces power. What's on the other side of the wire fence?"

He hesitated. I swung my arm back and caught him with open palm across the side of his face.

"What's the other side of the wire fence?"

"The boss-ape we met—we keep his enemies behind there—other tribes."

"Oh, he's your ally!" I said to Candida as I handed her the folded portal, "Rastell told me once there was no finer state than a slave state. This is a slave world—low-grade slaves, it's true, but amenable to discipline. Here you can rear slave armies to twitch through to your own matrix and assist in quelling rebellions—entirely expendable ape-armies. Right Rastell?"

I twisted his arm and enjoyed doing it.

"They have to suffer for righteousness' sake," he said.

I took the gun from Candida and stood up. He

started to rise and I told him to stay where he was in the mud. He propped himself on one elbow and lay glaring up at us—twice as dangerous as the boss-ape, I thought.

My sister-in-law was shivering. She clung to my free arm, looking away from Rastell.

"Why did he want us here, in this awful place?"

"Someone has to train the ape-army. Am I right, Rastell? And you'd like revenge on me. You are no fugitive from your world. They need cynical minds like yours, don't they, to maintain their beastly status quo?"

He lay in the mud without speaking, the folds of his mouth bitter.

I said, "I was destined to guard the apes while your other exiles here trained them, wasn't I, Rastell? Something menial like that!"

With some of his old spirit, he said, "Only those we trust get easy jobs like guard duty. For the rest, there are plenty of dirty jobs. Someone has to swab out the ape-barracks."

He got up very slowly, watching me, his face gray, blood running over his cheeks and chin. He rubbed it away as if it were dirt.

"What are you going to do with him, Sherry?"

"I'll have to shoot him, won't I?"

"Yes, you'll have to shoot him."

I was nerving myself to do that. Unfortunately, I had to look into his square sullen face. How little I understood him! I had seen him in bravery and fear. Rastell fought to maintain the iniquitous systems of his own matrix (as we all instinctively did), yet he had muttered of the slaves here that they were better left as they were. He was both a hypocrite and a believer. No, I couldn't sum him up—and perhaps the easy confidence with which we gauge a man's character is never possible when wide cultural differences lie between us.

I couldn't sum him up. Equally, I couldn't kill him.

"Give me the key to the gate across the stream, Rastell."

He shook his head. "I haven't got a key."

"Hold the gun on him, Candida, while I search him!"

Rastell gestured defeatedly. Saying nothing, he unzipped a tunic pocket, pulled out a large key, and tossed it to me. I caught it, putting it in my own pocket without comment.

The rain ran down his face in spasmodic drops, and he made no attempt to brush them away. I gestured at him with the gun.

"Go back to the village," I said. "The boss-ape will look after you until someone comes to rescue you."

Rastell stared fixedly at us. He opened his mouth as if to speak. Then he made the sign of the cross and turned away, beginning to walk slowly back along the way we had come. Candida and I watched him go.

The rain was increasing now. Clutching the portal and the gun, we worked the ferry across the stream. I helped Candida up the slippery bank and we unlocked the gate. It led into a rank scrubby field; as we mounted the slope, the great enclosure beyond was revealed.

Despite the drizzle, there were ape-people moving in squads—marching, I suppose you would say. They were watched over by black-uniformed men: victims, no doubt, of Rastell's regime, who would be more than pleased to shelter us. Curtains of rain, sweeping over the tiny figures, part-revealed, part-concealed gaunt concrete buildings behind, stretching like barracks before a line of fir trees.

God knows, it was far from being a cheering prospect. Yet the sight of human misery and struggle—animal and spiritual always intermixed—seemed to reassure us in this strange place by its very familiarity. So Candida and I clutched each other's hands and trudged toward the gray buildings.

No doubt they would offer more than shelter. More than bread.

Over them, streaming water, a gigantic cross.

Faith in ferroconcrete.

Intangibles, Inc.

"Always seems to be eating time in this house," Mabel said.

She dumped the china salt- and pepper-shakers down at Arthur's end of the table and hurried through to the kitchen to get the supper. His eyes followed her admiringly. She was a fine figure of a young girl; not too easy to handle, but a good-looker. Arthur, on the other hand, looked like a young bull; none too bright a bull either.

"Drink it while it's hot," she said, returning and placing a bowl of soup before him.

Arthur had just picked up his spoon when he noticed a truck had stopped outside in the road. Its hood was up, and the driver stood with his head under it, doing no more than gazing dreamily at the engine.

Arthur looked at his steaming soup, at Mabel, and back out of the window. He scratched his scalp.

"Feller's going to be stranded in the dark in another half-hour," he said, half to himself.

"Yep, it's nearly time we were putting the lights on," she said, half to herself.

"I could maybe earn a couple of dollars going to see what was wrong," he said, changing tack.

"'This is food like money won't buy or time won't improve on,' my mother used to say," Mabel murmured, stirring her bowl without catching his eye.

They had been married only four months, but it had not taken Arthur that long to notice the obliquity of their intentions. Even when they were apparently

119

conversing together, their two thought-streams seemed never quite to converge, let alone touch. But he was a determined young man, not to be put off by irrelevancies. He stood up.

"I'll just go see what the trouble seems to be out there," he said. And as a sop to her culinary pride, he called, as he went through the door, "Keep that soup warm—I'll be right back!"

Their little bungalow, which stood in its own untidy plot of ground, was a few hundred yards beyond the outskirts of the village of Hapsville. Nothing grew much along the road except billboards, and the stationary truck added to the desolation. It looked threadbare, patched and mended, as if it had been traveling the roads long before trains or even stagecoaches.

The overalled figure by the engine waited till Arthur was almost up to it before snapping the hood down and turning around. He was a small man with spectacles and a long, long face which must have measured all of eighteen inches from crown of skull to point of jaw. In among a mass of crinkles, a likable expression of melancholy played.

"Got trouble, stranger?" Arthur asked.

"Who hasn't?" His voice, too, sounded like a màss of crinkles.

"Anything I can do?" Arthur inquired. "I work at the garage just down the road in Hapsville."

"Well," the crinkled man said, "I come a long way. If you pressed me I could put a bowl of steaming soup between me and the night."

"Your timing sure is good!" Arthur said. "You better come on in and see what Mabel can do. Then I'll have a look-see at your engine."

He led the way back to the bungalow. The crinkled man scuffled his feet on the mat, rubbed his spectacles on his dirty overalls, and followed him in. He looked about curiously.

Mabel had worked fast. She'd had time, when she saw through the window that they were coming, to toss their two bowls of soup back into the pan, add water, put the pan back to heat on the stove, and place a clean apron over her dirty one.

"We got a guest here for supper, Mabel" Arthur said. "I'll light up the lamp."

"How d'you do?" Mabel said, putting out her hand to the crinkled man. "Welcome to our hospitality."

She said it just right: made it really sound welcoming, yet, by slipping in that big word "hospitality," let him know she was putting herself out for him. Mabel was educated. So was Arthur, of course. They both read all the papers and magazines. But while Arthur just poured over the scientific or engineering or mechanical bits (those three words all meant the same thing to Mabel), she studied psychological or educational or etiquette articles. If they could have drawn pictures of their idea of the world, Arthur's would have been of a lot of interlocking cogs, Mabel's of a lot of interlocking school marms.

They sat down at the table, the three of them, as soon as the diluted soup warmed, and sipped out of their bowls.

"You often through this way?" Arthur asked his visitor.

"Every so often. I haven't got what you might call a regular route."

"Just what model is your truck?"

"You're a mechanic down at the garage, eh?"

Thus deflected, Arthur said, "Why, no, I didn't call myself that, did I? I'm just a hand down there, but I'm learning, I'm learning fast."

He was about to put the question about the truck again, but Mabel decided it was time she spoke.

"What product do you deal in, sir?" she asked.

The long face wrinkled like tissue paper.

"You can't rightly say I got a product," he said,

leaning forward eagerly with his elbows on the bare table. "Perhaps you didn't see the sign on my vehicle: 'Intangibles, Inc.' It's a bit worn now, I guess."

"So you deal in tangibles, eh?" Arthur said. "They grow down New Orleans way, don't they? Must be interesting things to market."

"Dearie me!" exclaimed Mabel crossly, almost blushing. "Didn't you hear the gentleman properly, Arthur? He said he peddles intangibles. They're not things at all: surely you knew that? They're more like—well, like something that isn't there at all."

She came uncertainly to a halt, looking confused. The little man was there instantly to rescue both of them.

"The sort of intangibles I deal in are there all right," he said. "In fact, you might almost say they're the things that govern people's lives. But because you can't see them, people are apt to discount them. They think they can get through life without them, but they can't."

"Try a sample of this cheese," Mabel said, piling up their empty bowls. "You were saying, sir. . . ."

The crinkled man accepted a square of cheese and a slab of home-baked bread and said, "Well, now I'm here, perhaps I could offer you good folks an intangible?"

"We're mighty poor," Arthur said quickly. "We only just got married, and we think there may be a baby on its way for next spring. We can't afford luxuries, that's the truth."

"I'm happy to hear about the babe," the crinkled man said. "But you understand I don't want money for my goods. I reckon you already gave me an intangible: hospitality; now I ought to give you one."

"Well, if it's like that," Arthur said. But he was thinking that this old fellow was getting a bit whimsical and had better be booted out as soon as possible. People were like that. They were either friendly or unfriendly, and unfortunately there were as many ways of being objectionable while being friendly as there were while being unfriendly.

Chewing hard on a piece of crust, the crinkled man turned to Mabel and said, "Now let us take your own case and find out which intangibles you require. What is your object in life?"

"She ain't got an object in life," Arthur said flatly. "She's married to me now."

At once Mabel was ready with a sharp retort, but somehow her guest was there first with a much milder one. Shaking his head solemnly at Arthur, he said, "No, no, I don't quite think you've got the hang of what I mean. Even married people have all sorts of intangibles, ambition and whatnot—and most of them are kept a dead secret." He turned to look again at Mabel, and his glance was suddenly very penetrating as he continued. "Some wives, for instance, take in into their pretty heads very early in marriage always to run counter to their husbands' wishes. It gets to be their main intangible, and you can't shake 'em out of it."

Mabel said nothing to this, but Arthur stood up angrily. The words had made him more uneasy than he would confess even to himself.

"Don't you go saying things like that about Mabel!" he said in a bull-like voice. "It's none of your business, and it ain't true! Maybe you'd better finish up that bread and go and see anybody don't pinch your truck!"

Mabel was also up.

"Arthur Jones!" she said. "That's not polite to a guest. He wasn't meaning me personally, so just you sit down and listen to a bit of conversation. It isn't as if we get so much of that!"

Squelched, Arthur sat down. The crinkled man's long crinkled face regarded him closely, immense compassion in the eyes.

"Didn't mean to be rude," Arthur muttered. He fiddled awkwardly with the salt shaker.

"That's all right. Intangibles can be difficult things to deal with—politeness, for one. Why, some people never use politeness on account of it's too difficult. The only way is to use willpower with intangibles." He sighed. "Willpower certainly is needed. Have you got willpower, young man?"

"Plenty," Arthur said. The crinkled man seemed unable to understand how irritated he was, which of course made the irritation all the greater. He spun the salt shaker at a furious speed.

"And what's your object in life?" persisted the crinkled man.

"Oh, why should you worry?"

"Everyone's happier with an object in life," the crinkled man said. "It don't do to have time passing without some object in life, otherwise I'd be out of business."

This sounded to Mabel very like the maxims she read in her magazines, the founts of all wisdom. Pleasure shared is pleasure doubled; a life shared is life immortal. Caring for others is the best way of caring for yourself. Cast your bread upon the waters: even sharks got to live. Mabel was not too happy about this little man in overalls, but obviously he could teach her husband a thing or two.

"Of *course* you got an object in life, honey," she said.

Honey raised his bovine eyes and looked at her, then lowered them again. A crumpled hand slid across the table and removed that fidgeting salt shaker from his grasp. Arthur had a distinct feeling he was being assailed from all sides.

"Sure, I got objects ... make a bit of money ... raise some children ..." he muttered, adding, "and knock a bit of shape into the yard."

"Very commendable, very honorable," the crinkled man said in a warm tone. "Those are certainly fine objectives for a young man, fine objectives. To cultivate the garden is especially proper. But those, after all, are the sort of objectives everyone has. A man needs some special, private ambition, just to distinguish himself from the herd."

"I'm never likely to mistake myself for anyone else, mister," Arthur said unhappily. He could tell by Mabel's silence that she approved of this interrogation. Seizing the pepper shaker, he began to twirl that. "That yard—always full of chickweed...."

"Haven't you got any special, private ambitions of your own?"

Not knowing what to say without sounding stupid, Arthur sat there looking stupid. The crinkled man politely removed the twirling pepper shaker from his hand, and Mabel said with subdued ferocity, "Well, go on then, don't be ashamed to admit it if you've got no aim in life."

Arthur scraped back his chair and lumbered up from the table.

"I can't say any more than what I have. I don't reckon there's anything in your cargo for me, mister!"

"On the contrary," said the crinkled man, his voice losing none of its kindness. "I have just what you need. For every size of mentality I have a suitable size of intangible."

"Well, I don't want it," Arthur said stubbornly. "I'm happy enough as I am. Don't you go bringing those things in here!"

"Arthur, I don't believe you've taken in a word this...."

"You keep out of this!" Arthur told her, wagging a finger at her. "All I know is, this traveling gentleman's trying to put something over on me, and you're helping him."

They confronted each other, the crinkled man sitting nursing the two shakers and looking at the husband and wife judiciously. Mabel's expression changed from one of rebellion to anguish; she put a hand to her stomach.

"The baby's hurting me," she said.

In an instant, Arthur was around the table, his arms about her, consoling her, penitent. But when she peeped once at the crinkled man, he was watching her hard, and his eyes held that penetrating quality again. Arthur also caught the glance and, misinterpreting it, asked guiltily, "Do you reckon I ought to get a doctor?"

"It would be a waste of money," the crinkled man said.

This obviously relieved Arthur, but he felt bound to say, "They do say Doc Smallpiece is a good doctor."

"Maybe," said the crinkled man. "But doctors are no use against intangibles, which is what you're dealing with here. . . . Ah, a human soul is a wonderful intricate place! Funny thing is, it could do so much, but it's in such a conflict it can do so little."

But Arthur was feeling strong again now that he was touching Mabel.

"Go on, you pessimistic character," he scoffed. "Mabel and me're going to do a lot of things in our life."

The crinkled man shook his head and looked ineffably sad. For a moment they thought he would cry.

"That's the whole trouble," he said. "You're not. You're going to do nothing thousands of people aren't doing exactly the same at exactly the same time. Too many intangibles are against you. You can't pull in one direction alone for five minutes, never mind pulling together."

Arthur banged his fist on the table.

"That ain't true, and you can get to hell out of here! I can do anything I want. I got willpower!"

"Very well."

Now the crinkled man also stood up, pushing his chair aside. He picked up the pepper- and salt-shakers and plonked them side by side, not quite touching, on the edge of the table.

"Here's a little test for you," he said. His voice, though still low, was curiously impressive. "I put these two shakers here. How long could you keep them here, without moving them, without touching them at all, in exactly that same place?"

For just a moment Arthur hesitated as if grappling with the perspective of time.

"As long as I liked," he said stubbornly.

"No, you couldn't," the visitor contradicted.

"Course I could! This is my place, I do what I like in it. It's a fool thing to want to do, but I could keep them shakers there a whole year if need be!"

"Ah, I see! You'd use your *willpower* to keep them there, eh?"

"Why not?" Arthur asked. "I got plenty of willpower, and what's more I'm going to fix the yard and grow beans and things."

The long face swung to and fro, the shoulders shrugged.

"You can't test willpower like that. Willpower is something that should last a lifetime. You're not enough of an individualist to have that kind of willpower, are you now?"

"Want to bet on that?" Arthur asked.

"Certainly."

"Right. Then I'll bet you I can keep those shakers untouched on that table for a lifetime—my lifetime."

The crinkled man laughed. He took a pipe out of his pocket and commenced to light it. They heard spittle pop in its stem.

"I won't take on any such wager, son," he said, "because I know you'd never do it and then you'd be disappointed with yourself. You see, a little thing like you propose is not so simple; you'd run up against all those intangibles in the soul as I was talking about."

"To hell with them!" Arthur exploded. His blood was now thoroughly up. "I'm telling you I could do it."

"And I'm telling you, you couldn't. Because why? Because in maybe two, maybe five, say maybe ten years, you'd suddenly say to yourself, 'It's not worth the bother—I give up.' Or you'd say, 'Why should I be bound by what I said when I was young and foolish?' Or a friend would come in and accidentally knock the shakers off the table; or your kids would grow up and take the shakers; or your house would burn down; or something else. I tell you it's impossible to do even a simple thing with all the intangibles stacked against you. They and the shakers would beat you."

"He's quite right," Mabel agreed. "It's a silly thing to do, and you couldn't do it."

And that was what settled it.

Arthur rammed his fists deep down into his pockets and stood over the two shakers.

"I bet you these shakers will stay here, untouched, all my life," he said. "Take it or leave it."

"You can't," Mabel began, but the crinkled man silenced her with a gesture and turned to Arthur.

"Good," he said. "I shall pop in occasionally—if I may—to see how things are going. And in exchange I give—I have already given—you one of my best intangibles: an objective in life."

He paused for Arthur to speak, but the young man only continued to stare down at the shakers as if hypnotized.

It was Mabel who asked, "And what is his objective in life?"

As he turned toward the door, the crinkled man gave a light laugh, not exactly pleasant, not exactly cruel.

"Why, guarding those shakers," he said. "See you, children!"

Several days elapsed before they realized that he went out and drove straight away without any further trouble from the engine of his ancient truck.

At first Mabel and Arthur argued violently over the shakers. The arguments were one-sided, since Mabel had only to put her hand on her stomach to win them. She tried to show him how stupid the bet was; sometimes he would admit this, sometimes not. She tried to show him how unimportant it all was; but that he would never admit. The crinkled man had bored right through Arthur's obtuseness and anger and touched a vital spot.

Before she realized this, Mabel did her best to get Arthur to remove the shakers from the table. Afterward, she fell silent. She tried to wait in patience, to continue life as if nothing had happened.

Then it was Arthur's turn to argue against the shakers. They changed sides as easily as if they had been engaged in a strange dance. Which they were.

"Why should we put up with the nuisance of them?" he asked her. "He was only a garrulous old man making a fool of us."

"You know you wouldn't feel right if you did move the shakers—not yet anyhow. It's a matter of psychology."

"I told you it was a trick," growled Arthur, who had a poor opinion of the things his wife read about.

"Besides, the shakers don't get in your way," Mabel said, changing her line of defense. "I'm about the place more than you, and they don't really worry me, standing there."

"I think about them all the while when I'm down at the pumps," he said.

"You'd think more about them if you moved them. Leave them just a few more days."

He stood glowering at the two little china shakers. Slowly he raised a hand to skitter them off the table and across the room. Then he turned away instead and mooched into the yard. Tomorrow, he'd get up real early and start on all that blamed chickweed.

The next stage was that neither of them spoke about the shakers. By mutual consent they avoided the subject, and Mabel dusted around the shakers.

Yet the subject was not dropped. It was like an icy draft between them. An intangible.

Two years passed before the antediluvian vehicle drove through Hapsville again. The day was Arthur's twenty-fourth birthday, and once more it was evening as the overalled figure with the long skull walked up to the door.

"If he gets funny about those shakers, I swear I'll throw them right in his face," Arthur said. It was the first time either of them had mentioned the shakers for months.

"You'd better come in," Mabel said to the crinkled man, looking him up and down.

He smiled disarmingly, charmingly, and thanked her, but hovered where he was, on the step. As he caught sight of Arthur, his spectacles shone, every wrinkle animated itself over the surface of his face. He read so easily in Arthur's expression just what he wanted to know that he did not even have to look over their shoulders at the table for confirmation.

"I won't stop," he said. "Just passing through and thought I'd drop this in."

He fished a small wooden doll out of a pocket and dangled it before them. The doll had pretty, round, painted light blue eyes.

"A present for your little daughter," he said, thrusting it toward Mabel.

Mabel had the toy in her hand before she asked in sudden astonishment, "How did you guess it was a girl we got?"

"I saw a frock drying on the line as I came up the path," he said. "Good night! See you!"

They stood there watching the little truck drive off and vanish up the road. Both fought to conceal their disappointment over the brevity of the meeting.

"At least he didn't come in and rile you with his clever talk," Mabel said.

"I *wanted* him to come in," Arthur said petulantly.

"I wanted him to see we'd got the shakers just where he left them, plumb on the table edge."

"You were rude to him last time."

"Why didn't you make him come in?"

"Last time you didn't want him in, this time you do! Really, Arthur, you're a hard man to please. I reckon you're most happy when you're unhappy. You're your own worst enemy."

He swore at her. They began to argue more violently, until Mabel clapped a hand to her stomach and assumed a pained look.

This time it was a boy. They called him Mike, and he grew into a little fiend. Nothing was safe from him. Arthur had to nail four walls of wood around the salt- and pepper-shakers to keep them unmolested; as he told Mabel, it wasn't as if it was a valuable table.

"For crying out loud, a grown man like you!" she exclaimed impatiently. "Throw away those shakers at once! They're getting to be a regular superstition with you. And when are you going to do something about the yard?"

He stared darkly and belligerently at her until she turned away.

Mike was almost ten years old, and away trapping birds in the woods, before the crinkled man called again. He arrived just as Arthur was setting out for the garage one morning, and smiled engagingly as Mabel ushered him into the front room. Even his worn old overalls looked unchanged.

"There are your two shakers, mister," Arthur said proudly, with a gesture at the table. "Never been touched since you set 'em down there, all them years ago!"

Sure enough, there the shakers stood, upright as sentries.

"Very good, very good!" the crinkled man said, looking really delighted. He pulled out a notebook and made an entry. "Just like to keep a note on all my customers," he told them apologetically.

"You mean to say you've folks everywhere guarding salt shakers?" Mabel asked, fidgeting because she could hear the two-year-old crying out in the yard.

"Oh, they don't only guard salt shakers," the crinkled man said. "Some of them spend their lives collecting matchbooks, or sticking little stamps in albums, or writing words in books, or hoarding coins, or running other people's lives. Sometimes I help them; sometimes they manage on their own. I can see you two are doing fine."

"It's been a great nuisance keeping the shakers just so," Mabel said. "A man can't tell how much nuisance."

The crinkled man turned on her that penetrating look she remembered so well but said nothing. Instead, he switched to Arthur and inquired how work at the garage was going.

"I'm head mechanic now," Arthur said, not without pride. "And Hapsville's growing into a big place now— yes, sir! New canning factory and everything going up. We've got all the work we can handle at the garage."

"You're doing fine," the crinkled man assured him again. "But I'll be back to see you soon."

Soon was fourteen years.

The battered old vehicle with its scarcely distinguishable sign drew up in front of the bungalow, and the crinkled man climbed out. He looked about with interest. Since his last visit, Hapsville had crawled out to Arthur's place and embraced it with neat little wooden doll's houses on either side of the highway. Arthur's place itself had changed. A big new room was tacked onto one side; the whole outside had been recently repainted; a lawn with rosebushes fringing it lapped up to the front fence. No sign of chickweed.

"They're doing OK" the crinkled man said, and went and knocked on the door.

A young lady of sixteen greeted him and guessed at once who he was.

"My name's Jennifer, and I'm sixteen, and I've been looking forward to seeing you for simply ages! And you'd better come on in because mom's out in the yard doing washing, and you can come and see the shakers because they're just in the same place and never once been moved. Father says it's a million years' bad luck if we touch them, 'cause they're intangible."

Chattering away, she led the crinkled man into the old room. It too had changed; a bed stood in it now, and several faded photographs hung on the wall. An old man with a face as pink as a sunset sat in a rocking chair and nodded contentedly when Jennifer and the crinkled man entered. "That's father's pop," the girl explained, by way of introduction.

One thing was familiar and unchanged. A bare table stood in its usual place, and on it, near the edge and not quite touching each other, were two little china shakers. Jennifer left the crinkled man admiring them while she ran to fetch her mother from the yard.

"Where are the other children?" the crinkled man asked father's pop by way of conversation.

"Jennifer's all that's left," father's pop said. "Prue the eldest, she got married like they all do. That would be before I first came to live here. Six years, most like, maybe seven. She married a miller called Muller. Funny thing that, huh?—A miller called Muller. And they got a little girl called Millie. Now Mike, Arthur's boy, he was a young dog. He was good for nothing but reproducin'. And when there was too many young ladies that should have known better around here expecting babies—why, then young Mike pinches hold of an automobile from his father's garage and drives off to San Diego and joins the navy, and they never seen him since."

The crinkled man made a smacking noise with his

lips, which suggested that although he disapproved of such carryings-on he had heard similar tales before.

"And how's Arthur doing?" he asked.

"Business is thriving. Maybe you didn't know he bought the garage downtown last fall? He's the boss now!"

"I haven't been around these parts for nearly fifteen years."

"Hapsville's going up in the world," father's pop murmured. "Of course, that means it ain't such a comfortable place to live in any more.... Yes, Arthur bought up the old garage when his boss retired. Clever boy, Arthur—a bit stupid, but clever."

When Mabel appeared, she was drying her hands on a towel. Like nearly everything else, she had changed. Her last birthday had been her forty-eighth, and the years had thickened her. The spectacles perched on her nose were a tribute to the persistence with which she had tracked down home psychology among the columns of her perennial magazines. Experience, like a grindstone, had sharpened her expression.

Nevertheless, she allowed the crinkled man a smile and greeted him cordially enough.

"Arthur's at work," she said. "I'll draw you a mug of cider."

"Thank you kindly," he said, "but I must be getting along. Only just called in to see how you were all doing."

"Oh, the shakers are still there," Mabel said, with a sudden approach to asperity, sweeping her hand toward the pepper and salt. Catching sight as she did so of Jennifer lolling in the doorway, she called, "Jenny, you get on stacking them apples like I showed you. I want to talk with this gentleman."

She took a deep breath and turned back to the crinkled man. "Now," she said. "You keep longer and longer intervals between your calls here, mister. I thought you were never going to show up again. We've had a very good offer for this plot of ground, enough money to set us up for life in a better house in a nicer part of town."

"I'm so glad to hear of it." The long face crinkled engagingly.

"Oh, you're glad are you?" Mabel said. "Then let me tell you this: Arthur keeps turning that very good offer down just because of these two shakers sitting here. He says if he sells up, the shakers will be moved, and he don't like the idea of them being moved. Now what do you say to that, Mr. Intangible?"

The crinkled man spread wide his hands and shook his head from side to side. His wrinkles interwove busily.

"Only one thing to say to that," he told her. "Now this little bet we made has suddenly become a major inconvenience, it must be squashed. How'll it be if I remove the shakers right now before Arthur comes home? Then you can explain to him for me—eh?"

He moved over to the table, extending a hand to the shakers.

"Wait!" Mabel cried. "Just let me think a moment before you touch them."

"Arthur'd never forgive you if you moved them shakers," father's pop said from the background.

"It's too much responsibility for me to decide," Mabel said, furious with herself for her indecision. "When you think how we guarded them while the kids were small. Why, they've stood there a quarter of a century. . . ."

Something caught in her voice.

"Don't you fret," the crinkled man consoled her. "You wait till Arthur's back and then tell him I said to forget all about our little bet. Like I explained to you right back in the first place, it's impossible to do even a simple thing with all the intangibles against you."

Absentmindedly, Mabel began to dry her hands on the towel all over again.

"Can't you wait and explain it to him yourself?" she asked. "He'll be back in half an hour for a bite of food."

"Sorry. My business is booming too—got to go and see a couple of young fellows breeding a line of dogs that can't bark. I'll be back along presently."

And the crinkled man came back to Hapsville as he promised, nineteen years later. There was snow in the air and mush on the ground, and Arthur's place was hard to find. A big movie theater showing a film called *Lovelight* bounded it on one side, while a new six-lane bypass shuttled automobiles along the other.

"Looks like he never sold out," the crinkled man commented to himself as he trudged up the path.

He got to the front door, hesitating there and looking around again. The garden, so trim last time, was a wilderness now; the roses had given way to cabbage stumps; old tickets and ice-cream cartons fringed the cinema wall. Chickweed was springing up on the path. The house itself looked a little rickety.

"They'd never hear me knock for all this traffic," the crinkled man said. "I better take a peek inside."

In the room where the china shakers still stood, a fire burned, warming an old man in a rocking chair. He and the intruder peered at each other through the dim air.

"Father's pop!" the crinkled man exclaimed. For a moment he had thought. . . .

"What you say?" the old fellow asked. "Can't hear a thing these days. Come here. . . . Oh, it's you! Mr. Intangibles calling in again. Been a durn long while since you were around!"

"All of nineteen years, I guess. Got more folk to visit all the time."

"What you say? Didn't think to see me still here eh?" father's pop asked. "Ninety-seven I was last

November, ninety-seven. Fit as a fiddle, too, barring this deafness."

Someone else had entered the room by the rear door. It was a woman of about forty-five, plain, dressed in unbecoming mustard green. Something bovine in her face identified her as a member of the family.

"Didn't know we had company," she said. Then she recognized the crinkled man. "Oh, it's you, is it? What do you want?"

"Let's see," he said. "You'd be—why, you must be Prue, the eldest, the one who married the miller!"

"I'll thank you not to mention him," Prue said sharply. "We saw the last of him two years ago, and good riddance to him."

"Is that so? Divorce, eh? Well, it's fashionable, my dear—and your little girl?"

"Millie's married, and so's my son Rex, and both living in better cities than Hapsville," she told him.

"That so? I hadn't heard of *Rex*."

"If you want to see my father, he's through here," Prue said abruptly, evidently anxious to end the conversation.

She led the way into a bedroom. Here curtains were drawn against the bleakness outside, and a bright bedside lamp gave an illusion of cosiness. Arthur, a *Popular Mechanics* on his knees, sat huddled up in bed.

It was thirty-three years since they had seen each other. Arthur was hardly recognizable, until you discovered the old contours of the bull under his heavy jowls. During middle age he had piled up bulk which he was now losing. His eyebrows were ragged; they all but concealed his eyes, which lit in recognition. His hair was gray and uncombed.

Despite the gulf of years which separated their meeting, Arthur began to talk as if it were only yesterday that they had spoken.

"They're still in there on the table, just as they always were. Have you seen them?" he asked eagerly.

"I saw them. You've certainly got willpower!"

"They never been touched all these years! How ... how long's that been, mister?"

"Forty-five years, all but."

"Forty-five years!" Arthur echoed. "It don't seem that long—shows what an object in life'll do, I suppose. Forty-five years—that's a terrible lot of years, ain't it? You ain't changed much, mister."

"Keeps a feller young, my job," the crinkled man said, crinkling.

"We got Prue back here now to help out," Arthur said, following his own line of thought. "She's a good girl. She'd get you a bite to eat, if you asked her. Mabel's out."

The crinkled man polished up his spectacles on his overalls.

"You haven't told me what you're doing lying in bed," he said gently.

"Oh, I sprained my back down at the garage. Trying to lift a chassis instead of bothering to get a jack. We had a lot of work on hand. I was aiming to save time. Should have known better at my age."

"How many garages you got now?"

"Just the one. We—I got a lot of competition from big companies, had to sell up the downtown garage. It's a hard trade. Cutthroat. Maybe I should have gone in for something else, but it's too late to think of changing now.... Doctor says I can get about again in the spring."

"How long have you been in bed?" the crinkled man asked.

"Weeks, on and off. First it's better, then it's worse. You know how these things are. I should have known better. These big gasoline companies squeeze the life out you. Mabel goes down every day to look after the cash for me. Look, about them shakers...."

"Last time I came, I told your lady wife to call the whole thing off."

Arthur plucked peevishly at the bedclothes, his hands shining redly against the gray coverlet. In a moment of pugnacity he looked more his old self.

"You know our bet can't be called off," he said pettishly. "Why d'you talk so silly? It's just something I'm stuck with. It's more than my life's worth to think of moving those two shakers now. Mabel says it's a jinx, and that's just about what it is. Move them and anything might happen to us! Life ain't easy, and don't I know it."

The long head wagged sadly from side to side.

"You got it wrong," the crinkled man said. "It was just a bet we made one night when we were kind of young and foolish. People get up to the oddest things when they're young. Why, I called on some young fellows just last week—they're trying to launch mice into outer space, if you please!"

"Now you're trying to make me lose the bet!" Arthur said excitedly. "I never did trust you and your Intangibles too much. Don't think I've forgotten what you said that first time you come here. You said something would make me change my mind, you thought I'd go in there and knock 'em off the table one day. Well—I never have! We've even stuck on in this place because of those two shakers, and that's been to our disadvantage."

"Guess there's nothing I can say, then."

"Wait! Don't go!" Arthur stretched out a hand, for the crinkled man had moved toward the door. "There's something I want to ask you."

"Go ahead."

"Those two shakers—although we never touch 'em— if you look at them you'll see something. You'll see they got no dust on them! Shall I tell you why? It's the traffic vibration from the new bypass. It jars all the dust off the shakers."

"Useful," the crinkled man said cautiously.

"But that's not what worries me," Arthur continued. "That traffic keeps on getting worse all the time. I'm scared that it will get so bad it'll shake the shakers right off of the table. They're near the edge, aren't they? They could easily be shaken off, just by all that traffic roaring by. Supposing they are shaken off—does that count?"

He peered up at the crinkled man's face, but lamplight reflecting from his spectacles hid the eyes. There was a long silence which the crinkled man seemed to break only with reluctance.

"You know the answer to that one all the time, Arthur," he said. It was the only time he ever used the other's name.

"Yep," Arthur said slowly. "Reckon I do. If them shakers were rattled off the table, it would mean the intangibles had got me."

Gloomily, he sank back onto the pillows. The *Popular Mechanics* slid unregarded on to the floor. After a moment's hesitation, the crinkled man turned and went to the door; there, he hesitated again.

"Hope you'll be up and about again in the spring," he said softly.

That made Arthur sit up abruptly, groaning as he did so.

"Come and see me again!" he said. "You promise you'll be around again?"

"I'll be around," the crinkled man said.

Sure enough, his antique truck came creaking back into the multiple lanes of Hapsville traffic another twenty-one years later. He turned off the bypass and pulled up.

"Neighborhoods certainly do change fast," he said.

The movie theater looked as if it had been shut down for a long time. Now it was evidently used as a furniture warehouse, for a big pantechnicon was loading up divans outside it. Behind Arthur's place, a block of ugly apartment buildings stood; children shrieked and yelled down its side alley. On the other side of the busy highway was a row of small stores selling candies and pop records and the like. Behind the stores was a busy helicopter port.

He made his way down a narrow side alley, and there, squeezed behind the rear of the drugstore, was Arthur's place. Nature, pushed firmly out elsewhere, had reappeared here. Ivy straggled up the posts of the porch, and weeds grew tall enough to look in all the windows. Chickweed crowded the front step.

"What do you want?"

The crinkled man would have jumped if he had been the jumping kind. His challenger was standing in the half-open doorway, smoking a pipe. It was a man in late middle age, a bull-like man with heavy, unshaven jowls and gray streaking his hair.

"Arthur!" the crinkled man exclaimed. And then the other stepped out into a better light to get a closer look at him.

"No, it can't be Arthur," the crinkled man said. "You must be—Mike, huh?"

"My name's Mike. What of it?"

"You'd be—sixty-four?"

"What's that to you? Who are you—police? No—wait a bit! I know who you are. How come you arrive here today of all days?"

"Why, I just got around to calling."

"I see." Mike paused and spat into the weeds. He was the image of his father and evidently didn't think any faster.

"You're the old pepper-and-salt guy?" he inquired.

"You might call me that, yes."

"You better go in and see ma." He moved aside reluctantly to let the crinkled man squeeze by.

Inside, the house was cold and damp and musty. Mabel hobbled slowly around the bedroom, putting things into a large black bag. When the crinkled man entered the room, she came close to him and stared at him, nodding to herself. She herself smelled cold and damp and musty.

She was eighty-eight. Under her threadbare coat, she had shrunken to a little old lady. Her spectacles glinted on a nose still sharp but incredibly frail. But when she spoke her voice was as incisive as ever.

"I thought you'd be here," she said. "I said you'd be here. I told them you'd come. You would want to see how it ended, wouldn't you? Well—so you shall. We're selling up. Selling right up. We're going. Prue got married again—another miller, too. And Mike's taking me out to his place—got a little shack in the fruit country, San Diego way."

"And . . . Arthur?" the crinkled man prompted.

She shot him another hard look.

"As if you didn't know!" she exclaimed, her voice too flinty for tears. "They buried him this morning. Proper funeral service. I didn't go. I'm too old for any funerals but my own."

"I wish I'd come before. . . ." he said.

"You come when you think you'll come," Mabel said, shortly. "Arthur kept talking about you, right to the last. . . . He never got out his bed again since that time he bust up his back down at the garage. Twenty-one years he lay in that bed there."

She led the way into the front room where they had once drunk diluted soup together. It was very dark there now, a sort of green darkness, with the dirty panes and the weeds at the windows. The room was completely empty except for a table with two little china shakers standing on it.

The crinkled man made a note in his book and attempted to sound cheerful.

"Arthur won his bet all right! I sure do compliment him," he said. He walked across the room and stood looking down at the two shakers.

"To think they've stood there undisturbed for sixty-six years. . . ." he said.

"That's just what Arthur thought!" Mabel said. "He never stopped worrying over them. I never told him, but I used to pick them up and dust them every day. A woman's got to keep the place clean. He'd have killed me if he found out, but I just couldn't bear to see him believing in anything so silly. As you once said, women have got their own intangibles, just like men."

Nodding understandingly, the crinkled man made one final entry in his notebook. Mabel showed him to the door.

"Guess I won't be seeing you again," he said.

She shook her head at him curtly, for a moment unable to speak. Then she turned into the house, hobbled back into her dark bedroom, and continued to pack her things.

Since the Assassination

She had no sensation of falling.

In perfection, she rode the thin air down, her body in a curiously exultant attitude as she plunged toward the blue American earth, controlling her rate of fall by the slightest movements of neck and head.

In these tranced moments, she almost lost the sense of her own identity. She was pleased to strip off her character, always feeling it inadequate. Because of that, skydiving had become first a consolation then an obsession; she was too remote from herself to be other than remote from her husband, Russell Crompton, Secretary of State. And since the assassination of the President, a month ago, the vast new burdens he had had to shoulder—burdens foreshadowing the future—had driven them even further apart.

So every day she flung herself from his private plane, snatching seconds of a rapture immeasurable on terrestrial time scales. I feel now the future in the instant.

Those seconds were compressed with luminous comprehensions, hard to grasp when the skydive was over, when she was confined to earth. In the city one knows not the great hinterland. She understood that a new epoch was about to emerge—on the ground, little men without wisdom sought to deliver it, just as they sought to find the assassin, rating one task no higher than the other. Her husband also hoped to be strong and great on these points, but, in her reading of his character, she denied him the ultimate power. She knew a man who had that kind of power—Jacob

Byrnes, Jake, hero, victim, clown, seer—and spoke his name secretly into her breathing mask. His thought reaches me.

Her great swoop through the upper air had brought her to 2,250 feet. Now her relationship with the ground was an imminent one, and she pulled at her ripcord to release the first parachute; her equipment was of the simplest, as if she liked to keep this miracle natural.

Below her grew the drop zone, recently created in one corner of the Russell estate. Crompton was richer than Jake Byrnes, the craftier politician too, which was why he had survived where Jake had gone under. Why compare the two? She had Jake on her mind, had a sudden image of him—no, that did not make sense; these images of the future could not always be regarded as precognitive since perhaps more than one kind of time prevailed undetected in the universe: but the image clearly showed her welcoming Jake into his own house. He had been injured in some way but was smiling at her. Curious; in their rare meetings, he seemed not to like her greatly.

Before she landed, square in the target area, she saw Russell was waiting for her, a lonely figure leaning against his black roadster, wearing the simple raincoat he affected when he was experiencing isolation and wanted to feel like one of the people.

He came toward her frowning, so that she was careful to avoid tumbles and to land on her feet. A last-moment spill of wind took her running toward him; Crompton had to put out a hand to stop her, steadying her by the shoulder.

"Rhoda! I thought I'd find you playing this game. I want you to come on a drive with me."

He was stern because he disliked this obsession of hers. A Freudian was Crompton, who liked in his relaxed moments to talk the straight jargon and explain grandly to Rhoda that she suffered from the death wish and was "really" trying to kill herself by this skydiving. With more oblique views on what was reality, she kept her own counsel; a reserved woman.

She took off her goggles and unzipped her leather suit. He could not but observe her red lips and the fine fair hair suddenly blowing free. A marvelous unreachable woman who irritated him at this moment because she would not ask where he wanted her to go.

"Get a shower and change, will you? I'm going to drive down to Gondwana Hills and consult Jacob Byrnes. I want you to come along."

Again he waited for her to sneer and ask, "So that I can defend you from your old flame Miriam Byrnes?" But she never sneered, never said the obvious. Maybe that was what he enjoyed about Miriam and her like; when politics had grown so complex, women should remain simple. Did this one read his thoughts? He looked away, frightened about his own transparency; nervous illness simmered inside him, manifesting itself in disquieting intuitions that others knew evil things about him; he felt himself trapped in a gothic entanglement of questioning. The robust wisdom of Byrnes would act like a salve.

"Is Jacob Byrnes back in favor?" she asked, as he walked with her toward the changing room.

"They're all calling him in this present trouble. If only we could find the killer, get the reporters off our necks, get behind shelter, stop this glare of public scrutiny. . . . I figure it might pay to see him. I want him to meet . . . never mind that. My office tells me even Vice-President Strawn rang him the day before yesterday."

President Strawn, she thought; the demotion must be meaningful. She shucked off her suit and strode naked into the shower; let him look.

Whatever happened, she too wished to see Byrnes. The image was healthful.

The little dictation machine stood silent for nine

minutes before former Secretary of State Jacob
Byrnes completed his sentence. In that while, Byrnes's
heavy and capable mind had hunted over a wide
range of topics past and present, docketing them,
methodically cataloging and compressing them into
the inadequacy of words. At last, setting down the
cigar, he said "... conclude—*have* to conclude that
the present is an epoch in which the new relationship
between man and the universe remains, for the rea-
sons above outlined, merely incipient. This is the
central factor...."

His central factor, at least. This vast memoir, designed in the first place to vindicate his forced retire-
ment from the government and clear away the old
scandals of ten years ago, had turned into a philosophical search; personal aspects had been lost, sunk in
oceanic thinking. The pauses between sentences, the
bouts of research, grew longer, Grigson's fingers above
the dictation machine more idle, as Byrnes pressed
hotly on, growing nearer the truth. He knew he was
getting nearer; the secret something that prevented a
brave new universal relationship from forming
pressed down on him and on his whole estate here at
Gondwana Hills, bringing him churning images, ran-
dom snatches of possibility.

"What was that, Grigson?"

" 'The central factor,' sir." The secretary masterfully
obliterated his own personality, crushed by the
Byrnes dollars, unable to crystallize into his own potential. Byrnes, who lived by empathy, derived only a
blank from the man, and often longed to hit him. He
had done so once, when plagued by something Miriam had done. Grigson had taken it well, of course.

"Central factor operating on the collective conscious. A breakthrough into a higher consciousness has
been aborted by the unfavorable crosscurrents of mid-
twentieth century, resulting in the waking nightmare
of inappropriate politico-economic systems imposing
themselves all over the globe. The cold war and the

Vietnamese War must be regarded as faulty psychic frameworks through which favorable developments are eclipsed by unfavorable ones."

Still dictating, he rose and went onto the wide balcony. There was a microphone here; no chance of Grigson not hearing. He liked to stand here and dictate, with the hills in the distance, the private landing field, and, nearer, the ornamental lake. Nearer still were the essential adjuncts to the house, such as the gymnasium, his son Marlo's squash court, the stables, and the swimming pool, which lay against the broad terrace with its statuary. They were laid out in an arrangement that did not please Byrnes, although he had been meticulous with the architects about the matter; but the spatial relationship remained in some way mediocre. He lifted up his eyes to the hills. That, at least, was ok. Even the line of the toll road was being erased year by year as the trees grew up. Not that he has so many more years.

Miriam was swimming in the pool. "Hi!" she called, and he signaled back. There was still communication on the nonresonant level, which maybe counted for something after ten years. She swam in the nude now, her depilated body gold brown under the water; somehow, he had ceased to worry about the staff looking on. He had even caught Grigson peeping. The tough guys on the guard force were the most nuisance, but Byrnes had long since conceded to himself that, in view of his wife's feeble mental equilibrium, her need to exhibit herself was better not repressed. Poor little Miriam: however much she stressed the invitation, what she had to offer was pitifully ordinary.

There was more mess around the area than usual. Marlo had some contractors in, an interior decorating firm, messing around with something there, some new project. His schizoid son's projects were always a sort of art therapy; as the search for a self-cure grew more desperate, the projects seemed to grow more elaborate. Byrnes hesitated to intrude on his son's sufferings and saw very little of him nowadays. Bad empathy there. He caught a flickering feeling—one of his images—for a sort of lunar environment, hurriedly repressed an image of his cold first wife, Marlo's mother, Alice. Just as well Miriam saw more of Marlo than he did, although he could not imagine what they said to each other.

Grigson was on the phone. He came out onto the balcony and said, "Private car at lodge, sir. Russell Crompton, the Secretary of State, wants to speak with you."

"Let him drive up. Inform Captain Harris in the guardroom."

"Yes, sir." The only sort of affirmative statement Grigson ever made.

So Russell Crompton was calling. Ever since the President's assassination, his scared successors had been phoning and radioing Byrnes. He was back in favor. It gave him some kind of guarded satisfaction, he realized. But they were all too nervous of bugging and spying to speak out. Now here was Russel Crompton, once a close friend, rolling up at his front gate! There was a nationwide search for a scapegoat, if not the killer; maybe he'd hear more about that. His particular philosophical beliefs led him to believe that the President's assassin must be a fellow countryman; the aborted universe relationship would not allow anything less specific. His stomach churned a little. The more one knew, the less it became!

"No more dictation, Grigson."

Grigson smiled and nodded, picked up his brief case, and left the room. For a moment, Byrnes lingered on the balcony, surveying the scene which was so shortly to be disturbed. Some things were of such immense value, like the peace of Gondwana Hills and the streams of thought that passed through his own mind; those were of value to him, nourished him, maintained his interest in life, and he hoped that when they were transfixed on to paper they would nourish some other people.

But personal relations also still occupied him. It was a multivalue system in which he enjoyed maneuvering, in winning and losing points; nor was his enjoyment entirely intellectual. He liked people as he still liked life.

Nor was he too old to feel that he wanted to be seen again at best advantage by Russell Crompton when the latter arrived. Not as an aging semischolar, a learned buffoon, but a jolly old political man still able to live it up as a bit of a playboy. He'd go down to the gym.

And why—he asked himself this as he crossed the room, taking a last glance at the precious muddle of his creation—why did he want to act a role with Russell? Russell, for all his faults and weaknesses, was always direct, never pretended, though he schemed; Byrnes never schemed—well, there had been occasions—but loved to pretend. But his playboy role with Russell was almost intended to be seen through; perhaps the real defense was against Russell's wife, the rather enigmatic Rhoda.

He wondered what his strong empathic sense would make of her this sunny day. That skydiving woman ... funny habit for a woman to take up. Beautiful hair. Something told him she would be accompanying Crompton, unlikely though that seemed.

But he was going to have to talk affairs of state.

Moving in his solid way, making himself more heavy than he in fact was, Byrnes crossed the corridor, took the elevator down to ground floor, and moved out into the blazing sun, stripping off his linen jacket as he went. He had a gun strapped around his waist, being a little afraid of assassination: or, alternatively, of not being able to kill himself, should he want to.

"Miriam!" he yelled, crossing by the pool.

"Hi! Coming in, Big Daddy?" She waved a brown arm languidly to him.

Screw that stupid name! "Get out and get dressed. Secretary of State Crompton is on his way up."

"Oh boy, Fancy Pants! Does he think we're hiding the Prexy-killer here? Will he want you to run for President? Is Rhoda coming with him?"

He passed stolidly on, through the ornate stone screens, imported from Italy and now covered with Russian vine, and made for the gym, flinging his jacket over a hook, and working away at pushups, his face purple. He was a solidly built man on the summer side of fifty-nine, and he was not going to let Crompton think he was past it. He meditated about his stomach as it touched the floor at regular and straining intervals. The viscera. That was where he felt things. Not a great intellectual man, but a great feeling man. That's what he had been, and almost nobody had guessed, except that bitch Alice, his first wife, who had taken full advantage of it. Even in his office he had to protect himself from the anger of others: it communicated their sickness to him; he was a stable man, wrecked by the storms about him.

You're an oddball, he thought. Few men he could really talk to. But his own company was not disagreeable. Crompton, too, was still by way of being a friend, wasn't he? Strawn too, come to think of it.

Nose to the ground, he thought of Rhoda again, vexed at himself for doing so. Oh no, Russell would not bring that strange, silent creature, surely? But the image told him she was near.

The image took on life. She was standing among bushes; he was very frightened. She was saying, "We have to cease to rely...." On what? The image was gone as soon as it was there: "... on logical systems"; or had he supplied that himself? After all these years, he still did not know how to deal with these moments of insight; which could only mean that his life pattern had set wrongly long ago, maybe in childhood; he could not take full advantage of the benefits offered by these extrasensory glimpses.

He stood up, morose. Living was so wonderful, his own faulty faculties were so wonderful; what he needed was a wise man or woman who could discuss such high matters with him. Still in his vest, he moved to the gym door. Crompton's big black Chrysler was just rolling up to the front of the house, Russell himself driving. Rhoda was in the back.

On their way back to the barroom, the two men ran through a few preliminary sparring platitudes. The bartender mixed them two tumblers of martini and was dismissed.

"I don't know why you want to see me, Russell, but did you have to bring your wife along?"

"Same old grumpy Jacob! You have good nags here, and she can go for a gallop. She thought she'd like to see Miriam."

"Rhoda and Miriam have nothing in common, and you know it. You afraid you've got to keep an eye on her all the while?" He was talking in this vein, he realized, because he was grumpy and had no strong urge to hear Crompton's confidences; the assassination, the troubles of the country, were things over which he had no jurisdiction and which no longer took precedence over his meditative life.

"Why don't you like Rhoda? She likes you."

He had wanted someone to talk to and here someone was, the Secretary of State, no less. Why not say it straight out and see what happened, forgetting the fact that Russell was plainly burdened with responsibilities and guilts and worries, and therefore a bad audience? "I am an empath, Russell; I pick up other people's emotions as easily as if I had an antenna on my head. Your wife's eyes always disconcert me. They tell me things I don't want to know, about her and about myself. Look, the future is aborting before our eyes, all the big promises not getting realized; it is creating a barrier of universal mental sickness. Empaths are more sensitive to what's in the air than others. I'm telling you, all our values are false, Russell, false! If. . . ."

"That's what I came to talk to you about," Crompton said. "A time foul-up. I agree the priorities are wrong, but I'm in a position to know what the priorities are. A lot of very nasty things have come up this week, things that only the President and one or two men under him knew of." He took a hefty drink of his martini.

"Things? You mean projects?"

"Sort of. Two in particular. God, Jake, I shouldn't be talking to you about them. They are so secret—well, they are so terrible—that either one of them alters man's relationship to his environment for good and all."

This came too alarmingly near to the subject of this morning's chapter in the masterwork. Brushing that reflection aside, Byrnes asked, "Why *are* you talking to me about them, then?"

"I happen to believe that there is a lot of sense in all the philosophical nonsense you talk. I feel I need to hear some of it today. Plus the fact that your bartender is one of the world's great artists."

They stared at each other. It was a hard, tricky world. You had to seek your allies where you could. Although there was some residual evil tinging Crompton's aura, Byrnes said, "If I can help, I will."

"We could be bugged here. Let's walk outside." He swallowed the rest of his drink.

"Bugged? Me, in my own place? The hell with that!"

"I'd feel better outside. I'm claustrophobia inclined—too many years in Washington."

Leaving the glasses, they walked through into the sunlight again, through the wide glass doors over which internal steel shutters could close at the touch of a flip switch. The decorators over in the squash court were making a noise with their machines; otherwise all was silent. The guards lounged in their glass boxes; no birds flew. As the two men walked along the terrace, they caught sight of Miriam and Rhoda riding on ponies toward the hills, Miriam in a turquoise bathing suit. Why had Miriam been so quick to get Rhoda (or herself) out of the way?

"We'll walk around the lake—if it isn't too far for you."

"Of course it isn't too far for me," Byrnes said. "The years pass more healthily here than in Washington." He felt his gun uneasily. There was always something about to materalize, sweeping down from the concealed headwaters of the past, deeds already committed in men's minds that manifested themselves like projections from the future; the present was a shock wave between past and future.

When they seemed to him to be far enough from the house, Crompton started talking. The Administration had been taken by surprise by the death, as if death were an amazing thing. There had not been a strong Vice-President to take over effectively, as Truman and Johnson had done on previous occasions of crisis. Strawn was already proving ineffectual as President. And there had been the secret projects. Some were already almost an open secret among the top men, the usual routinely sinister affairs of the overkill philosophy, such as new missiles and new strains of virus that could incapacitate whole populations. There was a top-secret antigravity research station on the moon, a fleet of interstellar probes in the works in California. But the really burdensome things were none of these. They were two other projects; one had some connection with the antigravity moon station, Crompton said. The other was called Project Gunwhale.

"Gunwhale? Gunwhale? What's that?"

"I can't tell you, Jake. I can only say. . . ."

"If you can't tell me, why come here and bring up the subject?"

"The questions it raises are so enormous. Metaphysical questions. Mankind is not ready to face such questions yet. I remember you said something to me once, somehow I remembered the phrase, about 'the eternal dichotomy of life.' The phrase stuck with me, and it just describes this Gunwhale Project. It seems on the surface to be one of the greatest blessings ever, yet it could easily prove the greatest curse. Its potential is so great—no, it can hardly be faced! We shouldn't have to face Gunwhale for at least two more generations."

"It's something like the A-bomb was in its time?"

"Oh no, nothing like that, nothing."

Byrnes exploded. "I don't plan to waste a whole precious day playing guessing games with you, Russell! Either you tell me or you don't tell me! Look, I'm as much a patriot as the next man, but since I was turned out of office, I'm doing my duty by thinking—thinking, goddamn it, the hardest job of work there is, thinking for all the guys who never think from one year to the next. Let me get back to my work or else tell me what you've got on your mind and let me help you."

Crompton was looking back, squinting in the sunlight and staring toward the two figures on horseback, who were cantering now. Casually, he said, "I back you still, Jake, when your name comes up, so it's only to you I'd say that your temper is the chief of your disqualifications from holding high office. And I wouldn't value the amateur thinking too high if I were you." He gripped Byrnes's arm. "You're a good guy, Jake, but you see we are all powerless."

"Never think it, never say it. Look at this view—man touched everywhere. God touched too, maybe, but shaped by man."

"I can't say anything about Gunwhale, though I'd like to do so. I'll tell you about the other chief headache we're landed with. One or two doctors and psychiatrists know about this, but they are under a security blanket, right under wraps. It's something that happened on the moon. Something that reveals that man's whole conception of the physical world—roughly what we call science—is going to have to be taken to pieces and rebuilt."

"It has to do with the antigravity research you mentioned?"

"Yes, but not in the way you would imagine. It's an effect the moon has on the research staff. Lunar gravity. Christ. . . . Look, I'll give it you straight. For the first time ever, eight men have just spent an appreciable time—six months—on the lunar surface, away from earth. They were relieved and brought back here last month, four or five days before the President was killed."

They were hidden from the house now. To afford shelter from the sun, a grove of bamboos had been planted, growing down to the lake, but Crompton seemed to avoid these, maybe thinking that they could be bugged. Byrnes stopped by the fishing pier, wanting to be still and listen as the Secretary of State went on.

"None of those eight men are normal any more. The moon has done something to their metabolism; physiologically and psychologically, they are something other than human."

"I don't get you. You can communicate with them?"

"With the utmost difficulty. To put the whole matter in layman's language—which is all I can understand in this matter—these moonmen are operating slightly ahead of earth time."

"Operating ahead . . . living ahead of time?"

"Ahead of earth time. Earth time is different from lunar time. They figure that each planetary body may have a different time."

Byrnes gave a laugh of disbelief. "You should tell that to Einstein."

"Never mind Einstein! Look, time is in some direct way related to gravity; that's what we've learned from our eight moonmen. Once you hear it, you shouldn't be too surprised. We've grown accustomed to thinking of earth as being down a great gravity well; it happens that it's also down a temporal well."

"So a time-energy equation is possible."

Crompton looked startled. "Nobody told me that. What do you mean, a time-energy equation?"

"Einstein's general theory has been suspect for some time; now his special theory will also have to be reexamined. But if his methods still hold good, then it may be possible to formulate a time-matter-energy relationship. Off the cuff, I'd say this paves the way for the H. G. Wells idea of a time machine. With computers to help us, a prototype could probably be constructed in a few months. What a vista!"

He stared at the younger man, saw that Crompton was lost, his mind involved in the nebulous machinery of government, not free to speculate, reluctant to make a step that seemed obvious to Byrnes. To get him back into his stride, Byrnes asked, "How did this temporal effect strike the men involved?" As he put the question, he felt a chill-like premonition coming over him; he glanced around, wondering what psychopathic patterns must whirl like furies above the heads of any men so involved with facing the impossible.

"The main effect might not have been noticed for years, but there is a side effect. Apparently, every living thing including man has built-in cellular clocks which keep pace with the daily revolution of the earth."

"Circadian rhythms."

"That's correct. You are more up on it than I am. I get no time for general reading. A long stay on the moon disrupts the cellular clocks. The clocks of this eight-man research team attempted to adjust to the period of a lunar day, which of course was impossible. They clicked over instead into Lunar Automatic, as I've heard it called. They are living .833 recurring seconds ahead of Earth Automatic. The effect now wears off at intervals, as customary gravity brings them back that .833 recurring seconds to terrestrial time. In those intervals, we can communicate with the men. Otherwise, they are schizoid or else seem not to be there at all."

The orchestra of the inner life ground forth its disharmonies. So the breakthrough into higher consciousness—the very phrase he had given Grigson that morning—the breakthrough was now on its way, the possibility of health was again offered, presenting itself paradoxically as sickness! Certain he was being watched, Byrnes swung around, pulling his gun from its holster. Someone was in the bamboo grove, crashing forward. He fired, a reflex of self-preservation. The charging image was a phantasm of himself, its mouth open, panting, its heavy old limbs jerking.

As soon as it was glimpsed, it was gone. As soon as Byrnes's shot was fired, the guard car started to roar forward; it sat continually on the landing field, engine ticking over. In fifteen seconds, the gunmen were piling out by Byrnes's side. Controlling his fury, Byrnes reassured them and told them to search the bamboo grove. He marched off with Crompton, knowing he would get no more out of the nervous fellow now, ignoring his questioning glance.

"Let me know if there is anything I can do on the moon question." His voice, he thought, had never sounded so helpless. What warning was that phantasm of the living trying to convey?

"It's essential to know what leading scientists will make of this time division," Crompton said. He was trembling from the surprise of his friend's shot; the specter of assassination, hiding still deeper fears, was always by him. "It's always a question of keeping off the damned reporters. Fetesti has just published a paper on the biochemistries of time; I want to get him in on this. Maybe we could have a top-level meeting with the scientists down here at Gondwana, without drawing too much attention to ourselves."

"Do that. I'll be glad to help." He knew it would be dangerous, without knowing why. The horrid sensational web of search, treason, and brutality, which always trailed off along its edges into drugs, perversion, lies, and suicide, was spreading once more across the continent; the endemic oppression pattern that sprang from the will-to-power in man's psyche and was always breaking out in new directions; it was the greatest disrupter of a healthful emergent future and could wreck this continent as it had Africa; Byrnes had been caught in its web ten years back; he wished to keep it from Gondwana Hills. "This whole place is at your disposal. My guard force would be glad of a real job to do."

"An Interim Committee has been set up. I'll put it to them." Plainly, that was all Crompton intended to say. Over his averted face fell opaque shadows, as his availability switched to shallower channels, away from the main streams of ego-anxiety.

As they walked toward the main buildings, Marlo came out of the squash court. He was a stringy youth of sixteen, wearing a dirty green Scandinavian sweater and old jeans. He looked pale and ill. It was the first time Byrnes had seen him for several days. Miriam saw more of him than he did; what they had in common was beyond speculation, but at least she did not shun the child as once she had. But often he disappeared. He had taken to making long journeys, either on horseback or in his own sports car, since he was not certified; and those journeys were as unknown to his father as were the fevered excursions of his spirit.

"Marlo any better these days?" Crompton asked and then, as if guessing the answer to that, "Do you have in a resident psychoanalyst for him presently?"

"It doesn't work for Marlo. The last one tried to

cure him with some new drug, and that didn't work either."

"The boy needs Steicher, a very good man I know in Washington. Steicher would release his repressed ego-aggression." Crompton believed in all that but chose not to press the matter, to Byrnes's relief. He had had too much trouble from all the alienists he had engaged to help Marlo; the one before last, a guy from New York, had turned up with two mistresses, sisters.

Marlo hesitated; he almost seemed not to notice them, then moved slowly in their direction.

"The death of the President appears to have upset him. On a personal level, he seems to feel little yet; on the public level, he seems to suffer a good deal. Could be the personality pattern for the future, I guess, unless we solve a few problems. When things get too strong for him, he's completely in retreat."

"Steicher could help."

The weight of people in the world, the result of the population explosion, particularly oppressed the boy. Even the square miles of Gondwana did not seem to help things.

"We have to want external aid before it can help us." He was growing slightly afraid of his son.

Crompton said, "Rhoda said she dreamed about Marlo last night."

"Yes?" He hardly knew whether it was true.

Making himself smile as Marlo came up, he reached out his hand to the boy, but Marlo slid away, setting his head on one side, with a gesture that seemed faintly derisory.

"They are shooting whales with guns on the lake again, Jacob," he said. His voice was without animation; his gaze ran through his father. "Our dear relations, sad to relate. The blue whale is now extinct, except in the cerebral seas of the soul, and our lake."

"What are you having done in the squash court, Marlo?"

As the boy turned on his heel, his eyes just flickered slightly; his father seized on it as a gesture of invitation. Taking hold of Crompton's arm, to show no malice was borne, he steered him after the boy, who was heading toward the court; the court had been a present for Marlo's fourteenth birthday; Marlo had played only one game of squash there but had spent many periods living almost entirely in the court, decorating it in various bizarre styles—each of which his psychiatrists had heralded as an advance toward normality.

Byrnes thought of that phrase, "advance toward normality," now, as he stood with Crompton and gazed at the cluttered interior of the court. The professional decorators had knocked off for lunch, and were drinking beer and eating sandwiches in the upper gallery. Below them, only half completed, was part of a lunar crater, with the star-blotched black of space behind.

Advance toward normality.... Just as well he had sacked the psychiatrists, operating like all psychiatrists on false premises: premises such as the notion of a received normality. As Crompton had just revealed, there was a new normality on the moon, where alien time trajectories could taint the human metabolism. And now Marlo was working toward that—like all artists, ahead of his time. But the moon mockup was like the sterile territory of death.

He had ceased to ask himself what it meant. But Crompton asked the question, looking decidedly uneasy.

"Just a coincidence," Byrnes said. "The lad's been reading space comics." But he had taken a whiff of illness off his son; or had he? Was he not getting whiffs of illness wherever he turned? An hour of crisis was approaching; the higher consciousness was about to be born, and he stood in the way of its midwives. The boy had disappeared among the builders' junk. He wanted a cigar and another drink.

The two men muttered and walked about and examined the foamed plastic that so closely resembled the cinderous dust of earth's satellite, uneasy in the presence of something they could not grasp. As they finally turned to the door, it was to discover their two women framed in the doorway.

"Gosh, are you both ok?" Miriam asked. "We thought we heard shots, and so we came back to see if anything was wrong. The guards say you saw someone in the grove, Jacob. Is that right? Are there spies around?"

She was almost a head shorter than Rhoda. She kissed Byrnes and gave Crompton a peck as well, as usual meaning nothing she said or did, Byrnes reflected. It could not be said of the alarm she expressed so prettily that it was either real or feigned. "So long since we saw you, Russ, and I keep telling Rhoda I know you have a great big state secret to tell Jacob, but that's just an excuse and really you came down to see me."

"You look good in your swimsuit, Miriam," Crompton said.

"You like it? It cost a packet! Isn't it pretty material?"

Rhoda said nothing. She was terrific in her silence, Byrnes thought; good waves came from her. She was slightly larger than he cared for a woman to be, but her skin and her small, well-shaped breasts ... well, that was a line of country he no longer found it profitable to pursue; philosophy was at least partly designed to keep that sort of stuff at bay. He went toward her, conscious of how objectionably he always behaved toward her. A masked attitude. He suspected she really knew how he felt about her; but if she had that amount of sensibility and perception, then why did he need to put on a performance, like an adolescent? Why did adolescents need to put on performances, come to think of it? Sometimes whole civilizations became involved in attitudes. The Japanese *haragei*, using attitudes as veils which were only occasionally intended to be impenetrable, saying things that were not meant. The inescapable and gigantic paradox of human behavior: gigantic, yet so petty. He wanted to make a note, wanted that more than the cigar or the drink.

He was standing staring at Rhoda. She stared back, entirely without defense or offense.

"Still doing the skydiving?" Her obsessive hobby was leaping from planes; *Life* had carried an article on her.

"Uh-huh. Still doing the memoir?"

He was still inwardly bothered about the moon thing. Without smiling, he said, "Maybe I get the same kicks out of philosophy you get out of free fall."

"You two should compare kicks some time," Miriam said, shrilly. "Jacob, take Rhoda in for a cocktail while I show this crazy setup to Russ."

"He's seen it." But he was glad of the excuse. On the whole, he felt women remained private even amid public affairs; it was a vanishing talent. As he led the silent woman away, he sought for ways to shed the *haragei* mask, but she seemed as remote as ever. Almost as if she had more in common with Marlo than with him. It roused his curiosity to visualize her poised in some kind of hallucinatory dream, ten miles above earth's surface; something of that transfixed state lingered around her still.

"He hates me, you know," Miriam told Crompton, as soon as Byrnes and Rhoda had disappeared. "I cut him off from public affairs in his prime, and he can't forget it."

"He's better away from the in-fighting."

"Oh, Russ, don't be stodgy with me, please. It's months since I saw you! I know you've got awful troubles with this assassination and all that, but I'm so lonely here. Even Marlo keeps vanishing."

"Where is the boy?" He was following her over the lunar mockup.

"He hides behind here. Marlo! Come out, darling! Really, he's getting nuttier than ever."

Marlo stuck his head out from behind a pillar and said, "You need to wear a time suit here. You walk with death. I create my own time and I defy death!"

Miriam looked at Crompton. The words seemed to have struck him a physical blow. "The boy knows!" he breathed. He turned and walked hurriedly away, out of the court, his hands spread in case he tripped over the equipment lying everywhere.

She followed, calling.

She hung on his arm. "The Secretary of State scared by a nut case! He's fun, Marlo's fun! I quite like him."

"Fun! He's talking about death ... and he seems to know about Lunar Automatic."

She chattered anxiously; he continued to look as if he had seen a ghost, indifferent when she led him in through the side entrance of the house, bustled the maids out of the kitchen, and brought him a beer out of the refrigerator. He drank with his head down, sighing between drafts.

"You are in a load of trouble or you wouldn't be down here at this time," Miriam said. "Tell me about it, Russ. Maybe a silly woman's insight would help."

"This place is bugged, I'll bet."

She laughed. "That's what I'm always saying." She put her hand over his hairy wrist, but he would not look at her. She slapped him.

"You men are so awful these days, so damned important! Look at me, Russ, am I so ugly now, so old? You used to fancy me. Have you no time for private affairs any longer?"

He switched on the transistor radio set in the counter and, under cover of the music, said, "Everything is in chaos back in Washington. Something's happened on the moon—well, it's technical and you wouldn't be interested. And another thing. Oh, my God! Just before he was shot, the President was going to activate a major project, Project Gunwhale. We've got to decide—more-than-ordinary guys should have to decide."

She giggled uncomfortably. "You don't think you are an ordinary guy. Don't fool with me. You know Jacob treats me with contempt—maybe rightly. Don't you cut me out entirely.... One more claim on you, you see! How was Europe, Russ?" He had been out of the country when the President was killed.

"Getting back to New York.... New York seems so old and incredibly burdened after those young capitals like London and Bonn and Copenhagen. Look, do something for me, Miriam. I don't really go along with these theories of Jake, but he is turning into a wise old man. He's mad, of course, shooting at phantoms, but maybe he has the greatest idea since the cavemen invented fire. Maybe it will now be possible to invent a time machine. He said something so valuable just now—threw it out. I'll give it equal priority with my other most pressing problems when I get back to Washington."

"Building a time machine?! I thought that was just a comic-book idea!" She laughed. "Isn't the world complicated enough without going into the future, or whatever you plan to do?"

"Maybe I was already thinking that. Look, all are agreed that right now world affairs have never been more snarled up. Ever since Hitler, nothing but terrible crises: the extermination of European Jewry, Stalin's purges, the H-bomb, the cold war, Korea, the population explosion, famines everywhere, Communist China. The pressure is not only from the past but from the future, from mouths unborn. Somehow, we have to make a breakthrough before we bog down into universal psychosis. A time machine could be a way—a marker buoy sent into future time, to get help or something—I don't know, I'm talking wild."

"Don't ask me to go into the future!"

For the first time, Crompton smiled at her with real

warmth and took her hand. "That's not what I want you to do for me. I begin to get a sort of superstition. I want you to keep a friendly eye on your stepson, Marlo. Suppose he says anything significant about the moon or time differences, or ... or people living for hundreds of years, will you note it down precisely and let me know?"

"Doesn't sound the sort of thing I'm good at." She made eyes at him.

"I don't want your note intercepted. Could you bring it to me in Washington personally?"

She looked soberly at him. "You do still love me a little, Russ. Of course, I'll do what you ask."

He stood up. "Thanks for the beer, Miriam. I'd better collect Rhoda. I have to be back for a conference at twenty hundred hours tonight."

The newscaster was saying, "Although the search for the late President's assassin or assassins has recently been stepped up to new levels, official circles in the capital are now admitting that hopes of an arrest are fading. Looks like this is destined to become one of the classic locked-room mysteries of all time. What did happen in the President's study, that evening of August eighteenth, just before dinner, while the President sat alone, studying—so it's said—an important document which is now rumored missing? Two of his personal guards sat in the corridor outside, within earshot, yet heard nothing. Here, for a latest opinion on the White House Mystery, is this station's special political correspondent. . . ."

Jacob Byrnes got up and walked out of the room, leaving Miriam sitting on the white velvet sofa, gazing at the screen. Like an invisible presence, Marlo hovered in the shadowed corner of the room. Turning, she called him over sharply, and he came, standing a few feet away.

"I have something for you, Marlo. You know what it is, don't you? Your weekly treat. Come nearer."

He hovered like a bird beyond the patch of lamplight, waiting to be enticed into the hand of its captor. She opened her purse and brought out a screw of paper, opening it so that he could see the cube of sugar it contained.

She gestured toward the TV set. "For all your funny ways, you dig quite a bit about what goes on in the world, don't you? Washington and Europe, I mean. How's life on the moon?"

He reached out a hand.

"How is life on the moon, Marlo?"

"I am not alone on the moon. Earth is my piece of desolation. Many people live where I live. My mother sent me there, long ago."

"It's cold on the moon."

"Cold and hot. More cold, more hot than here."

"Oh, cut the riddles, Marlo. Do you want this LSD or don't you? What do you mean, many people live on the moon?"

" ... mounting pressures which were driving the late President into a position of isolation. . . ." said the commentator.

"There has to be a place for unwanted people, or they die of famine or in concentration camps or hospital beds. No room in beds."

"And the President?" she asked, with sudden intuition.

Marlo shook his head. "He would have made it all worse. There are too many people already. When the moon is crowded, where do we all go then?"

She gave him the cube of sugar, and he retreated with it into the shadows. "It will do you no good! You're mad already, I suppose you know that?"

"Just ahead of my time," he said. "Otherwise there would be nothing. You are nothing. Even when you have all your clothes off, you are nothing." He put the white cube gently onto his tongue and closed his mouth; and then he stole quietly away.

Leaving the TV set to flicker in the empty room,

Miriam also got up, and walked down the wide silent corridor, lugubriously lit. Fortunately she believed in reincarnation; this life sure had its dull moments. She paused at the foot of the stairs and then mounted slowly, until she came to her husband's workroom. She rapped on the door and entered.

Byrnes was smoking a cigar. He nodded and said, "Grigson is just sorting some old movies I want to look through. Care to come down to the theater and see them?"

"Funnies?"

"Not funnies. Sobies. Documentaries or, in your language, dockies."

"Must you take the piss out of me all the time, Jacob? I come up here for a bit of company."

He did not answer. He was making notes on a pad while Grigson scuffled in the background.

"You're so busy, Jacob, so dull, shut yourself up here—you never even go fishing any more!"

"I went fishing not many weeks ago."

"That was last summer."

"So it was last summer, my darling."

He caught something in her face and said, "I'm sorry we don't talk more. I must try to produce this old think-piece of mine. I want to finish it by the end of the year—just the philosophy bit. To hell with the personal stuff—that's forgotten. No time for it."

"Everyone's obsessed with time."

"Ask yourself why."

"Oh, I know all that. Big crisis, big deal! Even Marlo's at it."

Now he was gathering up the day's notes that Grigson had typed out, absently fumbling for a pen to alter and correct and add. "'Battle between a higher plane of consciousness and a waking nightmare that . . .'—pretentious, but it will stand—Grigson, have you located that footage on the 1934 assassination of King Alexander of Yugoslavia yet?"

"No, sir."

"Hurry up!"

She stood in front of her husband and said, "Why are things worse than before? Are they objectively worse? Aren't you just getting old, Jacob?"

"Of course I am getting old! The personal memoir led me into this same question of things getting worse. It's a good question. Do you want a serious answer?"

"No, I just asked for a joke. Me, I'm never serious, am I?"

He caught her wrist as she was about to turn away. "I'm sorry to tease. I want you, Miriam. I must have some contact with the old world, and you must be it. Listen, I will give you your answer. It's not that things are getting permanently worse; it's just that this is crisis time, what in my book I call 'Clock-and-Gun Time.' Such crises have occurred before. There was one toward the end of the thirteenth century in Europe, when the towns were growing rapidly, creating new densities. New densities always imply new awareness. Guns and mechanical clocks were then invented, both originating from metalsmiths. Those two inventions brought deliverance from a philosophical impasse and paved the way to renaissance. Guns brought new spatial adventure throughout the world. Mechanical clocks, incorporating one of the world-changing inventions, the verge-escapement with foliot, were our first precision instrument and directed our inner landscapes toward more precise thinking.

"Those clocks sprang from Western society and molded it. They were no good to the civilized Chinese, whose society had so developed that to them mechanical clocks were little more than toys.

"The same thing may be happening today. Two radical new inventions or discoveries; Russell Crompton mentioned them. They might deliver us. Or they might strike us as no more than toys, marvels. Our imagination could fail before them. We need courage and imagination."

"That's what your book is going to give people?"

"You see the funny side of me, Miriam. Other people don't, so maybe I can help them."

She tickled him under the chin. "Don't do your pathos thing with me. It may have hooked me, but it won't keep me hooked. How is this gun-and-clock talk going to help anyone right now?"

"Isn't it still typical of the dichotomy running right through life? Guns are all externality and violence; clocks are all silence and inwardness. There you epitomize Western modes of thought, the ascendant mode on this planet now for several centuries. However bent we are on material things, we never entirely forget our hearts and minds. Okay, now we try at last to join them and reach a new conscious level. Damn it, woman, if the West doesn't do it, who else will?"

"Maybe you have a point there, honey. You are a wise old guy, I do know. Even Russ said so when he was here last week. By the way, I want to drive up to Washington tomorrow and do some shopping."

"That's why you're being nice to me! Grigson, where the hell is that newsreel?"

Grigson straightened, his face flushed, clutching a plastic spool. "I have it right here, sir."

"You're a paragon, Grigson. Miriam, give my love to Russell Crompton if you just happen to run into him, eh?"

Rhoda threw herself from the plane.

Her brain cleared at once. All the irresolutions and obscurities—the poverty of discussion on central things —lifted at once from her mind. At over 20,000 feet, Washington could be seen for the tiny thing it was in both the real and the subterranean affairs of man. And the earth itself: she saw the relationship now, one of magnificent cunning, as a problem that man had posed himself and was about to solve.

She spread herself, arms and legs bent backward, fixing the world with her mons veneris, adjusting her speed by the subtlest flection of the spine. From the fifth vertebra spouted ganglia, power, beauty, that charmed the knife-wind. It was the universal nerve center, counterpointed only by the blue American earth below.

She wore suit, mask, oxygen cylinder, packed two parachutes. This was her element. Rhoda was high.

There was no sensation of fall, no sensation of fear. Only the beatific equipoise of flight, the collusion with gravity and the forces of the universe, the eternity offered by two minutes of free fall. She had been on drugs, she had recently tried one of the luxury free-fall holiday schools set up between earth and Luna, where the very rich experienced psychedelic rapture between planets; but for Rhoda, the true kick came in riding the stratospheric layer just beyond the realm of her fellow beings.

In this tranced state, she could catch some of the stronger thoughts floating up to her. It always encouraged her to find that only pure or creative thoughts rose this high; the bad ones, of which there were plenty, stayed at around 2,500 feet, just before she pulled the ripcord. Which was as if the medievals had caught a glimpse of that curious scientific fact in their vision of a heaven above and a hell below. Good thoughts breathed hydrogen, the basic substance of the universe. Up here, the all-state manhunt had no being, having no purpose.

She encountered the thoughts of retired Secretary of State Jacob Byrnes; they were rich in hydrogen these days. They penetrated her body. He was troubled. She had no lover. Her husband's thought never touched her here. She had her raptures. She was, she thought, of the future, and so had an interest in seeing it healthily born. Jake was of the past, a dinosaur with love, absurd, heroic. He would die seeing the future enter the world.

This last thought Rhoda examined carefully and languidly as she volplaned down with the world between her thighs. Jake was troubled; he had discovered a sheet of paper. Without understanding what the paper was, she saw its tendrils spread all over the world. She would have to go to help him.

The skydive was finishing. She had been aloft immeasurable times, but now a confident circadian clock inside informed her that she was down to 2,250 feet. She needed no altimeter. As she reached inside her leather jacket for the ripcord, sick thoughts hit her. She caught a whiff of Marlo and knew many things. The parachute was opening; so was her whole area of perception, her mind painfully ripped open to an entirely new level of being, where all was revealed, flaming, frightening. . . .

Her old life on earth had ended. The plane that dropped her was not her husband's usual sports plane. A parascientific transference had been made; this plane had been—yes, they could not operate tied to earth, as Wells and the others had supposed—this had been a time vehicle, winging down out of space on the Byrnes-Fetesti time-energy equation, skimming through the stratosphere, coming as near as it dare to past-earth, depositing her for this one vital mission to insure the future was born unaborted.

Yes, from Russell's plane—they had wisely put her under artificial amnesia, but now it cleared—she had been captured from Russell's plane so long ago, carried into the future, trained, trained for this moment, brought back to the point in time from which she had been taken. And the impetus that made it possible for her to come back was the perception by old Jacob Byrnes that the discovery of time-wells along with gravity-wells made time travel practicable. She admired the symmetry of the design, even as she saw the terror that was to come in the next few hours. Spilling air, the sin-laden air of past-earth, she sank toward the drop zone.

"I wish to resign from my job, sir," said Grigson. "It has become anathema to me."

Byrnes was taken aback. "You don't like it here?"

"It is simply that you do not like me, sir, and I cannot tolerate it any longer." He stood rigid in a soldier's posture and had turned very pale.

Byrnes felt an immense shame. He could not face Grigson (what was his first name?); he had to go away, wander like an exile around his own estate. He had treated the man very badly, used his wealth, power, and charisma to purely ill ends, to defeat what little personality Grigson possessed. He had enjoyed doing it. He was an old, bitter, twice-defeated man; even at this moment, his wife, whose life he had blighted, was probably in the bed of one of his successors. No old bull of a herd had ever been so thoroughly routed.

And his son. . . . Had he ever cared that Marlo was isolated, out of touch? With some miserable and ill-defined intent of having a reconciliation with the boy (or at least humiliating himself again?), Byrnes made his way eventually to Marlo's quarters.

It must have been least two years since he was last in this wing of the building. That told of his neglect! But Marlo was by no means stagnating, whatever else he was doing. He had decorated this whole place, transformed the walls, with some sort of bright plastic stuff, some new material that created an illusory sense of projection, so that it seemed dangerous to walk along the corridor. There were montages, too, and meaningless phrases scrawled over the walls and ceilings. WHO KNOWS SPEAKS NOT. NATURAL DENSITY OF LIONS. LIFE REQUIRES MORE LIFE.

Life requires more life. It could be a warm or a cold thought. The appearance of warmth in the new decor might overlie a colder thing: a very frigid horror; such was the image Byrnes derived, although he could admit that the outward semblance was far more cheerful than he had expected. But he paused with his hand on the boy's study door, fearful of opening it, aware only of chill pouring forth at his viscera. Strange images of death. Of course, he was only an old man, failed politician, failed memoirist, failed philosopher. . . . But this was not personal death he felt radiating from the room; this was a general death, which included death for the unborn as well as the living. Sick to the stomach, Byrnes opened the door and walked in.

Russell Crompton had his face buried in the warm depilation of her flesh; nevertheless, he could not avoid hearing Miriam say, "But the guards who were outside the room—the guards must be involved in the murder."

It was the last thing Crompton wanted to discuss. He said wearily, "The FBI have virtually taken those two poor guys apart, and they didn't do it, period."

"Well, what was on this paper that got stolen off the President's desk? Is there a clue there? Was the assassin a foreign spy?"

"Look, honey, if you are fishing for a detective job, forget it. The missing paper is about something called Project Gunwhale—all very hush-hush. It's a top-secret memorandum concerning a certain pharmaceutical firm that has discovered a new drug which could change the whole social structure of mankind. If it turns up in the wrong place, wow!"

"Oh, another drug!" She sounded disappointed. This was, she reflected, the third Secretary of State she had lain with; how many girls could claim the same? She answered her own inward question: many more than you'd think, sweetie!

"Christ, I feel flaked out today. That conference on international affairs last night. . . . Many more weeks of this and we won't be able to stand the pace. It's not the work, it's the decision-making that kills you. Man is not a deciding animal."

"Philosophy I can get at home. Come and lie this

way, here. That's better! Tell me about these moon-men. I told you Marlo reckons he lives on the moon. Are your eight moonmen getting any better, because Marlo isn't?"

"You shouldn't feed him LSD, baby."

"I didn't mean to tell you that, Russ—you'd better forget it. Anyhow, Marlo likes LSD. It brightens him up. How are your moonmen? Tell me something sensational."

"Their condition is improving. They still flicker into invisibility occasionally, but that aberration grows less as their circadian rhythms adjust back to Earth Automatic."

She sat up. "Invisible? You mean you can't see them?"

"Not the ordinary sort of invisibility. It's just that when they are in the Lunar Automatic phase, they are actually .833 recurring seconds ahead of our time continuum and consequently cannot be experienced by our senses. Nothing to be scared of, and they'll soon be entirely back to normal, thank God."

She said, "I'm not scared; it's just—wait!" But her incoherence did not stop him; after all, men's elaborate affairs, so wonderful if punctuated by the simplicities of bed; he liked the full life, the intrigues within the Administration, liked everything, even the withdrawal of his wife, which gave him moral excuse for diversions like Miriam. He would rise refreshed and encouraged from the seamy bed as from the foam! Already, he was more anxious to talk than to listen, and scheming for possible political advantage from this newly discovered temporal disturbance. He was ready to get up and get back in there pitching, but out of politeness to an old flame he could chat and fondle for another ten minutes. Eight, maybe.

"Jake had the inspiration, saw at once that this implies entirely new possibilities for time-harnessing. I phoned Fetesti, who is a head man in the field, apparently, and he's coming to a conference in Washington this evening. A brilliant scientist, they say. Hungarian by origin. I don't want Jake to know I'm meeting Fetesti yet. ... I really ought to get dressed, pet. If the states could invent a time machine or a time projectile ahead of the rest of the world, that would solve most of our problems, huh?" He paused in the act of inserting his right foot in a sock and stared at her pale face. "You ok?"

"My God, Russ, I told you Marlo was carrying on about living on the moon and that it was a place for unwanted people to go."

"Useless, honey. You don't remember exactly what Marlo said. I told you to write it all down. Something half-remembered is useless."

"Ok, ok! But he was talking metaphorically. He didn't mean really on the moon. He meant lunar time." Suddenly, she clung to Crompton, and they nearly fell off the bed together. "You see—that's why Marlo never seems to be around. He is living in lunar time. He must have been in thought contact with the moonmen when they were carried back to earth, sick. Their sickness must have corresponded with his. He learned how to flip that little bit ahead. That's why he hardly ever seems to be around."

"Marlo, time-traveling? Impossible! What was that he said about the President? Try to remember!"

"Something about ... the President was going to make things worse, and there were too many people in the world already. ... Russ, you don't think it was *Marlo* did it? Not *Marlo?*"

Crompton pulled his pants on, keeping his face blank. "This is all in your head. It's just ego-aggression on your part, triggered by your guilt feelings because you get that little guy high on lysergic acid. If you could pin the assassination on him, why, you wouldn't have to feel bad at all. I know a good alienist here, guy called Steicher, specializes in repressed ego-aggression. He could help you. Why don't you go see him?"

She sat very still, staring ahead, not listening, and he noticed with some irritation that she was trembling. "The locked room—it would present no problem to Marlo if he could move that fraction ahead of time, emerging when he wanted to behind the President. He's acted odd ever since the moonmen came back. He's always away, you can't find him, he goes off in his car, nobody checks where he's been."

Putting a heavy hand on her shoulder, he said, "Look, Miriam, granted all that, why would he want to kill the President? What's the motivation?"

Then he remembered: Rhoda had dreamed about Marlo. He was frightened of Rhoda's dreams; they belonged to some super-reality which even Steicher could not satisfactorily explain away. Rhoda had dreamed that Marlo was playing the title role in a performance of *Macbeth*, which was held in the grounds of Gondwana. The boy had made a great Thane of Cawdor and had also played the part of the witches, which had much amused his father, Jake Byrnes. Byrnes enjoyed having his house cast as Macbeth's castle, but grew angry when his son insisted on ending the play on the lake, saying that the bamboo grove was moving in to destroy him.

Troubled by the dream, Crompton outlined it to Miriam. To his annoyance, she brushed it aside. "A dream means nothing; it's the facts that count. Besides, Rhoda's dream has no end."

"It did end! I remember. She said that Macbeth refused to be killed by Macduff—and the President was playing the part of Macduff!"

"Very cute! And Macbeth killed him instead of him killing Macbeth?"

He shook his head. "Funny, I remember I asked Rhoda that same question at the time. She did not know. These strange dreams of hers have their blanks. But it ended with Jake running out of the bamboo grove and killing Marlo."

They stared at each other. Miriam swallowed and

said, "You do think Marlo was the President's assassin, then?"

"There's the motive—he wanted to defeat Project Gunwhale, represented in the dream by Macduff's lineage. Its existence was a threat to his life."

"He had been to the White House as a boy, when his father was in the Administration. Maybe he could recall his way around. But a dream is just a dream."

"No more, no less. And when I spoke to the boy last week, he said something about shooting whales on the lake. His life is a dream. With the ability to move ahead of time, our precognition becomes for him preaction." As he spoke, Crompton felt some of the intense fear Marlo must have done, when looking at the thickening complexity of the future.

It communicated itself to Miriam. She said, "Russ, is Jake really going to kill Marlo? I'll have to stay here. I'm—I'm scared to go back to Gondwana."

Mentally disturbed or not, he was again the Secretary of State. Getting into his jacket, he said, "You believe in the actuality of symbolic levels too, don't you, Miriam? Stay here! But I'm getting down there with some police, fast. The whole nation wants that assassin *alive.*"

She seemed incapable of leaving the bed and was now cuddled down among the sheets, peering at him as he strode across the room as if she no longer recognized him. "Russ, you don't think that the drugs I've been giving him helped upset him in any way, do you? I really only did it to spite Jake a bit. I never meant. . . ."

As he picked up the telephone and began to dial, he said, "I forgot to tell you, honey. In the dream, you played Lady Macbeth."

The room was empty. At least, Marlo was not there. It took some while to verify the fact, because the room was so crowded with strange clutter that it baffled Byrnes's sight. He was still fighting the ill-feelings in his stomach.

The boy's sickness, it is antilife, he told himself. Just because such sickness is prevalent, we must not accept it as normal. It is a rejection. Sickness not the reverse of health but of moral responsibility.... People must be warned. Put it in the next chapter. Add that we have to come to terms with the way mental illness functions. After all, it has its own creativity. Illness is a mystery to us. As is health. The nightmares of sleep intrude into waking, and the horrors we face by day walk masked through the night. It's gun-and-clock time, when the orchestration of the inner life falters and the conductor absconds.

The bad images led him to one wall which was covered with recent newspaper clippings, a whole host, secured only along their top edges—the better to rustle and live, maybe—so recent they had not yet had time to yellow. All concerned the murder of the President. Several clips of the famous shot of him slumped over his desk. He had worked till the last—all very touching. You could see the flag behind his chair.

In the middle of the assemblage of fluttering columns was a white sheet of governmental memo paper. Byrnes recognized it at once and read it. He reread it. On the third reading, it made sense; and its place here also made sense. He clutched his belly.

It was a top-secret memorandum addressed to the late President by his advisers, subject Project Gun-whale. It advised that a comparatively obscure pharmaceutical combine, Statechem, Inc., had run a three-year test on a new type of gerontotherapeutic drug, patent name Surviva, with conspicuous success on seven species of laboratory animals. No animal showed signs of aging. Tests had also been carried out on human volunteers in the laboratory staff; although the test period was too brief for any positive results to be expected, all indications were hopeful: no signs of cellular deterioration—gray hair turning black—no deleterious side effects. Surviva seemed to promise extreme longevity and was inexpensive to produce. Permission was requested for Statechem to ask publicly for volunteers, and for the security blanket on its findings to be lifted. Statechem directors saw no reason why injections for immortality should not be available for all in ten months from the cessation of successful testing.

At the bottom of the memo, one of the President's advisers had written in longhand, "To go ahead with this in view of present world famines and overpopulation would shatter all social structures and wreck the whole planet in one generation."

Pinned to the memo was another sheet, an answer in what Byrnes recognized as the President's fluid italic script: "This is an old argument, Ted. If Statechem has it now, someone else will have it soon. We have to ok it and face the problems arising. Besides, we need the additional brainpower: imagine even an extra decade working life from every U.S. scientist. Besides, I'm irrevocably on the side of life." And his initials, slightly smudged. Must have been the last thing he ever wrote before the killer took him.

I'm irrevocably on the side of life. So am I, Byrnes told himself; can't help it. And immortal life? Well, you'd give it a swing. The resultant problems didn't bear thinking about; and the advisers, perhaps rightly, came out against the idea on that score. But the President, even more rightly, cut them down. Well, was going to cut them down when he was killed. By the initials of the advisers, Byrnes saw that Crompton and Strawn and two other men were involved. They would be no-sayers; and they were the ones now with the power.

And another thing. The killer. This was why he had killed. He would be a no-sayer. Saying no to life, no to the future, no to that terrible tide called progress; you

had to say yes and then *do* yes.... The killer had
killed and come away with this memo.

"Marlo? Where are you?" Marlo would be a no-
sayer. His insanity was one of his generation's major
ways of saying no. So he had given shelter to the
killer, housed the killer here, here in Gondwana Hills.
The painful irony of it! The old man felt his eyes
burn with tears. His own son sheltering the President's
assassin!

He dashed the tears quickly away and pulled out
his gun. Maybe the killer was still here. He crammed
the incriminating document into his pocket and
backed to the door. Wonderfully, the sick feeling had
left him. All he felt now was a blind anger, against his
son, against the killer, against the circumstances,
which he saw were reaching out again to involve him
in another disgrace; this one he could not withstand;
it would encompass his book, too, overwhelm its frail
merits and vital message. The future was dying, the
promise of the past collapsing into chaos.

"Come out, you bastards!" he bellowed. The gaudy
tangled room—thugs' hideout, nest of sickness, plot-
ter's parlor, den for a murderer—absorbed all sound.
It was full of the dull stained light he associated with
sin, a stain he had seen once in a university production of *Macbeth*. Light thickens and the crow makes
wing to the rooky wood. It frightened him a little. He
backed into the corridor again and roared his son's
name, as loud as he could, to bring his courage back.

Marlo appeared before him. One moment he was
not there, the next he was. Although his face was the
usual withdrawn blank, his eyes flared with purpose.
He moved toward his father, ignoring the revolver.
Byrnes was shouting at him, but it was as though
neither of them heard the noise. He got his arm
around his father's throat with a sudden movement
and pulled him back, violently, with an unexpected
hard strength. Stars swam in a red haze before
Byrnes's eyes, and his voice croaked off. He fought,

not understanding, the gun still in his hand, afraid even to hit Marlo with it.

Through the haze, he saw—or dreamed, it felt—Grigson run up, striking out with, of all futile Grigsonish articles, a leather briefcase. The briefcase caught Marlo hard under the eye. He at once let go of Byrnes, whimpering. Grigson, looking rather stupid, steadied himself for another blow; Byrnes sank to the floor, staring pitifully up. Marlo disappeared: flickered, vanished as if he had never been.

His senses came back. The idiot Grigson was pouring a little clear water on his face. Two servants were bending stupidly over him; there was a third man standing in the background. Byrnes roared and tried to get up. They assisted him.

"I heard your call for help, sir."

"You did a great job, Grigson!"

"But your son disappeared, sir, vanished like a ghost!"

"The hell he did! Call the guard! Did you call the guard?"

"No, sir!"

"You're fired, Grigson!"

"If you remember, sir. . . ."

"Go to hell!"

He staggered out, trying to orient himself. They had carried him to one of the bathrooms. Used to be Alice's bathroom . . . and that boy, Alice's boy, for him to attack his father, he must be hypnotized, in the power of a killer, an assassin, the assassin, hiding out in his place!

He hit the nearest alarm button and was comforted as the unholy babel broke out from the clock tower. He took the elevator down to ground level and was met at the gates by Captain Harris, head of the security team.

"Didn't you see I was being attacked over the bugging, Captain?"

"No, sir! Where were you?"

"In the west wing. I could have been killed! What were your men doing?"

"Your son removed all the bugging in that part of the house."

"Of course, he would have done.... Listen, Captain, get hold of my son. Don't hurt him, but hold him. Lock him up safe down here. He is sheltering the President's assassin. Yes, you heard me! Get that assassin if you have to burn the place down. No, no, don't do that! Have a man go straight and guard my study, in case anyone tries to get in there and wreck my work."

Harris nodded curtly. He lived for crises. He issued orders, dispatched the men efficiently, and told Byrnes, "All shuttering is down, sir, and all doors are on autolock. Nobody can get out without our say so."

"Ok." He was mollified at last, thanking God inwardly for Harris; Harris cared little about the future, but he was great for emergencies. "Then let me out here, will you? I need fresh air."

Harris deputized a younger man, who opened up the armor-plated front door and let Byrnes through. He staggered out and sat on his top step as the door closed behind him. He shielded his eyes and tried to calm his heartbeat, afraid of a stroke. His throat ached. The boy had hurt him.

It was growing dark. A dreary evening, the whole landscape Macbeth-colored, over the hills anger and unholiness. Good things of day began to droop and drowse. A searchlight came on over the lake on the landing field, picking him out. He stood up, feeling guilty and vulnerable, signaling to them to turn it off. The great eye did not waver. Byrnes fought an urge to hammer at the door behind him for readmittance.

His little English sports car stood by the house. Muttering angrily, he climbed in, started up, and drove across to the field, the beam following him all the way. They must have identified him, for a figure ran from the guard tower to meet him. It was Captain MacGregor, to whom Byrnes addressed a blistering stream of abuse.

"I'm sorry about that, sir," said MacGregor, without sounding very penitent. "Captain Harris explained the situation to me over the phone. We have an alert on out here. But Secretary of State Crompton just radioed, sir."

It was going to be bad. From men in office, full of ambition, only the worst could be expected. Death in their mouth; and in their eyes, dust. "Well?"

"He said your son is charged with murder, sir, and you are charged with complicity, sir."

"Washington madness! Madness!"

"He didn't radio from Washington, sir. He is flying over here, should be landing in eight minutes. Has strong police escort. Two planes. He ordered me personally to place you and your son under arrest, sir."

"MacGregor!"

"Sir?"

"I order you to shoot those planes down."

"Shoot. . . . I can't sir!"

"The future, man! The future demands it! Shoot them down!"

"I can't do that, sir. But equally I can't arrest you, sir. You're free till they land here, sir. It gives you seven or eight minutes to get away."

So MacGregor already judged him guilty. There was nothing he could do.

"Thanks, MacGregor."

He walked away, past the sports car, the engine of which still ran quietly, heading blindly toward the bamboo grove. So much for philosophy. That fool, Russell. So he and Marlo were to be made national scapegoats. A clever idea, certainly; much better than nabbing a complete unknown; they could fake it to look as if he had been after the Presidential seat himself, maybe—any madness they cared to dream up.

Miriam must have found out that Marlo was sheltering the assassin and had gone and told Russell Crompton. He would make political capital out of it.

Rhoda took his hand and said, "I'm here, Jake. Don't be alarmed."

"You, Rhoda? You, here? What are you doing at Gondwana?" The balm was still pouring from her, a lovely womanly emanation. She was standing on the spot where he had earlier fired at his own image; perhaps just a coincidence.

"I am on your side entirely, Jake. The future's side. I believe as you do that the world can only solve its problems by throwing them open and facing them, not by suppressing them. I also believe that it needs all the forces it can muster to do that, and that among those forces you personally are important—*and* that you will be lost, and your book with you, if you do not ride out this next ten minutes. I'll help on that. I know what is going to happen."

"Maybe you do."

" 'Here upon this bank and shoal of time, we'll jump the life to come.' But perhaps it invites ill-luck to quote Lady Macbeth!"

"Rhoda ... is the *haragei* gone? Can we speak and move freely together at last?"

"We can. I was not myself. Now I am."

"Well, I'm beside myself! I get only chill feelings from all but you. Maybe we should cease to believe in logical systems at the expense of all others. After all, machines are now freeing us from the necessity of either-or thought; that's their job; we should deal with the nusances, where real life lives. I intuit that Russell is going to make me a scapegoat on the national scale."

She nodded and said coolly, "You also realize that you are on the brink of madness. You must draw back. Russell has little against you save the guilt he feels for lying with your wife; but he has great ambition. To capture you and Marlo tonight and brand you with conspiring to kill the President would make him a national hero."

In the darkening sky, the sound of engines. The new jetcopters. Yes, their lights visible overhead. The birds of vengeance settling on the tender plains of peace.

"I must go to Marlo. He's mad! They must not hurt him!"

"Think! You are rejecting the evidence of your senses, preferring to embrace sickness rather than face truth. You saw Marlo vanish. You must admit that to yourself; and then you must admit another thing."

The darkness seemed to torment him. Angrily he shook his great gray head about, scattering tears. Trembling, he forced himself to say, "That *he* is the assassin."

For a moment he could not see. The bamboos boiled like a midnight ocean, and her words could scarcely reach him.

"Though the forces ranged against life are many, the thoughts of good always rise higher. Listen, my dear old battered Jake, you might clear yourself of complicity, but the disgrace would wreck you, break your life, disrupt the whole future course of events."

The copters were crawling down in their own winds now. She was shouting to make him hear. "I waited here for you because here you will see Marlo at any minute. He cannot maintain himself in the Lunar Automatic for long. He will run to shoot Russell, who—with Miriam's aid—has pieced together most of the information he needs for an arrest. Marlo has immense powers, but he is not supernatural. You do not need a silver bullet, Jake, to bring a better future into being."

He stared into her face. "You know I can't kill him, my son!"

She kissed him on the lips. "You will."

As the wind whipped around them and the two

black shapes of flight began to straddle the field, she pointed. "Your Captain Harris was too late with his lock-in! Marlo was already outside!"

Forgetting her, he hurried toward his son, a dark figure running at a crouch, using the dead ground behind the sports car to approach the machines now landing. He shouted, but Marlo did not hear. He grabbed him from behind.

To his sudden fear, he saw the knife in Marlo's hand and the blank stare in his eyes. A man like a machine, not so much sick as unable to feel human or feel for humanity. As the knife came around, Byrnes saw that Rhoda, calling aloud his own creed, was right: it was kill or be killed. Even so, he could not kill his own son: even survival had a relative value. He fired the gun down into the ground, three times, as fast as he could pull the trigger. It diverted Marlo only slightly. As the knife cut his side, Byrnes jumped on the boy's instep and punched him hard and wildly under the jaw. They tumbled to the wind-lashed ground together.

Jacob Byrnes refused to stay in the local hospital for more than a day. Bandaged tight, he got himself driven back to Gondwana Hills as soon as possible. A benevolent—a highly charged and erotic—image told him that Rhoda Crompton would be there.

As his driver helped him out of the car, Byrnes glared loweringly round. Work on the squash court had ceased, so there were no decorators about. But an army plane on the landing field, five big limousines, two police cars, and a mobile forensic laboratory told him that he had visitors. They would be taking poor Marlo's quarters apart, gathering every shred of evidence for the trial—in which, judging by yesterday's news reports, his father was going to be a sort of national hero as well as one of the chief witnesses. The wretched business would involve a colossal interruption of work; he thought he could face that if

Rhoda were around. His main efforts must be devoted to trying to help Marlo. Miriam could be helped through lawyers. Feeding drugs to the boy, feeding him drugs!—That took some forgiving!

At the top of the steps, Grigson met him.

"Mrs. Russell Crompton is inside, sir."

"Didn't expect to see you still here, Grigson."

"No, sir. But I thought you might have especial need of me over the next few months, in view of which I feel I should postpone my resignation a while."

He clapped his secretary on the shoulder. "We need you, Grigson. Help keep the cops out of my hair. We may need your dangerous briefcase again, for all I know. Come along!"

But Grigson faded away in the hall, muttering excuses, as Rhoda appeared. She had parachuted in and was carrying a pair of goggles in one hand, although she had changed into a corduroy dress. Her long ash hair was pulled into a single braid, which hung over one shoulder. Cutting through any reserve Byrnes might be feeling, she put her hands on his upper arm.

"You won't be surprised to see me, but I hope you're pleased. I figured you needed help here for a while."

"Everyone seems to think I need help. How intuitive everyone has suddenly become! Come on upstairs, Rhoda, before I go and talk to the cops. You can make me a drink; that damned hospital was on a temperance kick."

"How's the side?"

"It was a love bite." He looked at her, smiled, hoping he did not look too tired and old; she seemed to find a question in his gaze.

"I've finished with Russell," she said. "He, of course, has finished with Miriam, having got what use he can from her, so I suppose the situation is symmetrical."

"I ruined Miriam's life. I was too much for her. She's my responsibility; there is still help I can give, particularly now that Marlo is off my hands.... Rhoda, do they ... they don't make too much of a goddamned psychodrama of his trial, do they, purgation of national guilt and all that?"

She laughed. "I cannot foretell the future now. You defeated the predicted future the day before yesterday by not killing Marlo. So the laws of temporal causation must be reformulated—clearly *have* been reformulated in the time ahead of mine—as is shown by the way nobody travels back to a non-time-traveling age, for fear of altering temporal causation."

They took the elevator up to Byrnes's suite of rooms where he lived and worked. He still felt shy with her, had not entirely shed the feeling of *haragei;* he was inhibited from asking her directly what role she was going to play in his life. Knowing he was now, however undeservedly, a national hero for having tackled and disarmed his assassin-son, he felt his freedom curtailed. At least he could use the popularity while it lasted to promulgate the ideas he stood for. First, he must confer with Fetesti; Rhoda should sit in on that.

"You are going to be so necessary, Rhoda—not just personally. You don't have to ... return to whenever it is? You can stay?"

Coloring, she said, "Don't count on me too much, Jake. I love you, but I'm a skydiver and that's my first love—a sort of celestial junkie, you see. But I'll live here if you'll have me. Your drop zone is second to none."

She looked tenderly at the emotional warmth that crept into his face, then turned to get him a stiff drink as he sank into a chair, saying as she did so, "I have no place ahead. I was born thirty-eight years ago; the future that kidnapped me during one of my skydives was only twenty years ahead."

"It must be very different."

"Tremendously. And yet *you* would recognize it, if only because a small part lies already in your brain."

Should she go on and tell him? There were reservations in people, private even from themselves; she feared that what she was going to say might shock and startle him; but while it was his personal gun-and-clock time, so late in his life, he should have it straight. "Jake, while they were training me for this ... adventure ... they gave me the Surviva inoculations, a variety of the Surviva inoculations mentioned in that fatal memorandum to the late President. I'm not ... not subject to the usual three score years and ten any more."

There was a long silence in the room.

Finally, he scratched the top of his head and said, "People like you should always have the chance of a long, long life. I suppose that—twenty years ahead—I wasn't still lumbering around, doing good, holding forth, pontificating, was I?"

"... No. Your book was still holding forth, though, and doing good."

"Give us that drink! Then I don't have to decide; the decision has been taken. I don't want the inoculations. The trajectory of my life is something I refuse to wrench out of its pattern for anything." Suddenly he was frightened at what he had said. He had done too much, suffered too much—and there was more of that to be got through yet, of course. The pain of Marlo's trial. . . .

She kissed him as she handed him the glass. Suddenly he grabbed her with all his strength, only to release her, groaning.

"My side! I'll have at you, woman, when I'm healed."

"I hope so. Here's looking at you!"

"And you!" There was so much he wanted to ask. . . . That inestimable privilege, never before granted to any mortal, of being able to look coolly ahead to the evolving future. He must not abuse it, must take it in digestible portions. One of the first questions will have to be—maybe he should make a list—how they manage to square the population explosion with having people around for longer, if the world was not going to be unbearably clogged with living bodies. But, of course, if they adopted the only possible system and gave Surviva free to everyone proved capable of benefiting from extra years (and what sort of test would that be, O Lord!), then it needed only another serum mixed with the inoculations to guarantee that the immortals did not procreate, or only to a controlled degree. The technical problems were not so great; it was the social problems that loomed so very large. Even a better politico-economic system would change so much, the wars of aggression, the famines in one state while there were gluts in another. Since world decisions were now going to be made, and the future was once more out of the log pile, then clearly human consciousness was again on the dynamic upgrade toward a higher level of being. Longevity fitted naturally into the pattern. The pattern! Of course, that was what must be grasped—and could be grasped once the basic principle was taken—and the basic principle was so simple that the most backward African tribe embraced it wholeheartedly: life is good. And the clamor that would wake any day when Crompton announced the Surviva findings would show the West what the West had forgotten: that even sickness was precious, but life was better. Proof and proposition were all one; or to put it another way....

"Darling, you aren't drinking your drink!"

"I just want to make a note of something," he said.